Lyndon Publishing

Wanted
A Man For Christmas

Janice Olson

Lyndon Publishing

Wanted A Man For Christmas
Copyright © 2015 by Janice Olson

Requests for information should be addressed to:

Lyndon Publishing
2200 S. Smith Berry Rd., Suite 200
Pantego, Texas 76013
Website: www.LyndonPublishing.com

ISBN: 978-0-9764915-8-3

This book is a work of fiction. References to names, real people, characters, incidents, places, establishments, organizations, or locations are intended and are used fictitiously, and are the product of the author's imagination to provide a sense of authenticity. Any resemblances to actual events, locales, or persons, living or dead, are purely coincidental.

For more information about Janice Olson, please access the author's Website at: www.JaniceOlson.com, or email Janice@JaniceOlson.com.

Cover image, original photograph manipulated by Harry Olson, all rights reserved.

Lyndon Publishing Mission Statement:

To the best of our ability, publish, and distribute inspirational products that offer exceptional value and Biblical encouragement to the world while honoring God.

Forward

I dedicate this book to my terrific friends and beta readers, Jackie, Jewlene, Ann, Dana and Connie, who have given willingly of their time. All I can say is, you ladies are an awesome bunch of friends. You may not know this, but you make my life so much easier. ☺ Thank you and blessings for your hard work!

As always, I give thanks to God for the words and the stories, and to my loving husband Harry who puts up with "do you have time to listen to this?" He always does, thankfully.

And thank you to my loyal fans. Your joy of my books continues to inspire me. Your kind words are a balm to this writer's soul.

Wanted A Man For Christmas is Book Two in the Serendipity Series. Whitney's dilemma turns into a whimsical twist of fate. And like Whitney, when we least expect an answer, we find it's on the other side of the patio wall.

Before they call I will answer; while they are still speaking
I will hear. Isaiah 65:24 NIV

Enjoy the read.

Blessings,

Janice Olson

Wanted
A Man For Christmas

Chapter 1

I, Whitney Singleton, am in serious need of a man. Not just any man, but one who can clean up well and at least hold an intelligent conversation without blurting out … *yeah, right back at'cha dude*, or some other such dribble. And he can't be preening before a mirror or acting like he was doing me a favor being my escort.

Talk about desperate … that's me. And all because of the biggest event of my career—the Children's Hospital Christmas Benefit. Well, not mine personally, but for the charitable organization where I work.

Going over my options for the right man, I tapped my fingernail on the dining room table, my attention snagged by the Dallas skyline outside my high-rise apartment window. The long arms of darkness were creeping up the downtown buildings, snuffing out most of the light. And here I sat, no closer to a solution to my dilemma than I was this morning.

A dating service was out of the question. My friend, Sally Carlson, suggested one earlier this year. Been there, done that, and the experience was a total disaster. The service paired me up with three losers and then did their best to set me up with number four.

Bachelor No. 1 talked incessantly about his ten cats and his allergies. I listened, trying not to look bored while inconspicuously picking cat hair out of my food and mouth. Those little fuzzy pikers were relentless floaters, riding on the restaurant AC breeze into my food. Any other explanation for the cat hair would be unthinkable. Don't get me wrong, I love cats, but there is a limit when it comes to floating hair.

When I complained the next day to the woman at the dating service and asked for my money back, she apologized and hooked me up with Bachelor No. 2, or at least that's what I thought.

Bachelor No. 2 was the complete opposite of No. 1. The white space on his ring finger should have clued me in. He kept smoothing back his slick hair while giving me an extensive rundown of his finer qualities. When he said his wife didn't understand him, I barely held back from planting him a facer for being a two-faced cheater. Instead, I got up, walked out, and left him sputtering over how he shouldn't have to pay the whole restaurant bill.

Again, I complained to the dating service, asking for my money back. The woman guaranteed this time she had the perfect match or my money back, plus a $50.00 gift certificate.

Thinking the third time might be the charm, I agreed.

Bachelor No 3 was nothing like the other two. I had high hopes he might be a keeper. Good-looking, nicely

10

dressed, he treated me like a princess until it came time to say goodnight. That's when Prince Charming turned Sharktopus—half-shark, half octopus, nipping at my neck while feeling me up. To this day, I'll never know how his hands and arms could be everywhere at once.

I did my best to fight him off. Thankfully, I managed to pull the pepper spray from my purse, which I purposely carried for would be muggers and rapists. I figured this guy fit the bill. Lifting the little canister, I aimed and fired. Like a bucket of ice water to the face, his multiple arms dropped to his sides, he backed away wiping his eyes, swearing and calling me several choice names as he ran down the street.

The next day, while talking with Mary at the dating service—by now we had become bosom-buds—I drew the line when she suggested Bachelor No. 4. She had the nerve to say I was being picky and needed to consider the bad with the good.

I told her to send me a refund and the gift card for my trouble. Otherwise, I would turn the whole mess over to my lawyer, which I didn't have, but she didn't know that.

Dating service? Never again. I underlined the words.

For the umpteenth time, I scanned my list of scratched through names of probable escorts and my notations about each of them.

I double scratched through the names. The list dwindled down to my brother Seth, who I wouldn't ask, or my cousin Jed, who was out of the question. I loved Seth and Jed dearly, and they both had good manners and would clean up well, but I'd sooner show up alone than with a relative, especially a police detective or a parole officer.

Out of options, I pulled on my hoodie, slipped outside onto my balcony, and rested my arms on the railing. This time of evening was my favorite. The sunsets were generally spectacular and helped me wind down and clear my head from the day's clutter.

The white, mega-million-dollar Margaret Hunt Bridge, backed by rosy and gray clouds did wonders for my distraught mind. The serene scene took away some of my anxiety but not my problem.

"How bad could it be going alone?" I let loose a gusty, loud sigh, which felt good.

"That depends where you're going."

I nearly jumped over the railing, which wouldn't have been a good thing.

Jerking around, my hand to my throat, my insides quaked as if I'd been suspended over the side of my balcony, dangling twelve stories from the ground. I gave a sweeping glance in the direction of the voice. On the other side of the dividing half-wall of my balcony, I found the culprit that probably robbed me of a good ten years of life.

Adam Ryder sat studying me, his heels propped on a footstool, a beverage in his hand. He was the epitome of God's gift to women, especially with those dimples. At least he possessed all the outward appearances. Inwardly, he could be anything since I barely knew him.

"For Pete's sake, you nearly scared me to death." I lowered my hand. "Next time make a noise, like … clear your throat, cough, or shuffle your feet. Do something so a person will know you're lurking in the shadows."

His laughter zinged straight to my heart and gave me a fright of a different kind. It wouldn't be hard to fall for a guy like Adam.

"Sorry about that." His smile said differently. "You were in such deep thought, I didn't want to intrude. But when I heard you speak and didn't see anyone, I couldn't help myself."

I gave him a disgruntled look, willing my racing heart to settle down. My wayward pulse was harder to tame with his intent gaze directed at me.

"You're like my brother Seth. He's always trying to sneak up and scare me out of my wits."

"What can I say?" His brow rose then settled. "It's a male thing."

We both fell silent.

Fidgeting with the zipper on my hoodie, I wondered if I shouldn't go back inside before I did or said something stupid.

"Would you like to talk about it? Sometimes it helps. Sometimes it doesn't."

"Talk?" I scrambled for his meaning. "Oh, that. It's just a work matter. Nothing I can't handle." I returned my gaze to the skyline. *Where was my confidence earlier?*

I knew Adam well enough to exchange pleasantries. Our occasional meeting in the hall or in the stairwell were … *Hi, how are you? Fine thanks, and you? Not too bad. Have a nice day.* But more than that? … Zilch.

He rose and moved closer to the dividing wall where I stood. His mellow, woodsy cologne floated on the breeze, my senses coming alive.

The man was certainly easy on the eyes and definitely not a wimpy guy. In fact, he was more like a painting one could stare at for hours and still not see all the little hidden nuances the artist wanted the observer to find. The old cliché tall, dark, and handsome came to mind, but didn't quite do him justice.

Even shrouded by shadows, another look had me rethinking my earlier opinion of the man. He wasn't just handsome. He was a master's stroke of genius with his chiseled chin, cute dimples, and thick, wavy dark hair. An opinion I wouldn't dare voice aloud.

"I'm a good listener and not a bad problem solver if you'd like to bounce it off me."

When I was slow to answer, he shrugged and glanced away while taking a swig of tea or whatever was in his glass.

Spellbound, I watched his Adams apple ripple up and down as he swallowed.

13

Odd, I couldn't remember when, if ever, that little knot bobbing in a man's throat had been so hypnotically entertaining. The commercial of a man drinking deeply from a can while some of the contents flowed down his chin and over his bare, buffed chest popped into my head.

I slammed the door shut on the image as a blush worked its way up my neck to my face. To keep Adam from noticing, I turned my gaze back to the silhouette of the Dallas skyline. Now, cloaked in darkness, the city lights glimmered like diamonds in the blackened sky.

Call it foolhardy or just plain impulsive, truth is I wanted to spill my guts to this man.

"It-it's just this thing ..." Was I really going to open up to Adam? "It's a charity banquet my company puts on each year. It's coming up in three weeks. For the first time, I'm the organizer. And-ah ... well-ah ... I-I-ah ..." Babbling like a fountain, and to a complete stranger, no less. What was wrong with me? If I wasn't careful, I just might break out in song and dance, or cry on his shoulder.

"And you what?" He looked at me questioningly.

Though I tried, I couldn't stop the words from rushing out. "I find I'm without a date thanks to the low-life I was dating and his four-timing ways."

"Four-timing what?"

He had a cute way of scrunching up his nose.

"The guy was dating me and three other women at the same time. And just how pathetic does that make me sound?" I said the last under my breath.

Adam whistled through his teeth. "That guy must've had a death wish."

"Ya think?" I rolled my eyes. "I felt like doing him in myself, but restrained my baser instincts." I chuckled. "Mainly, because I didn't want to go to jail, and I already knew we didn't fit."

"That was big of you."

14

"Yeah, come to think of it, it *was,* wasn't it? The thoughts of tightening my hands around his scrawny throat didn't last more than a day or two."

He shook his head, his dimples appearing. "Remind me not to tick you off."

"I'll do that."

His laughter hung in the evening breeze, while his warm gaze wrapped around me and brought healing to my battered soul.

For the first time since Jeremy's cruel words, it felt good to have a man look at me with appreciation.

"I don't generally have violent tendencies but … I'm just saying." I shrugged with a saucy grin in place.

"I can tell. " He shook his head.

The quiet descended, causing me to want to flee back inside.

"And now, let me see if I understand your dilemma. You have a very important banquet to attend and don't have a date. How am I doing so far?"

"That about sums it up, except to say this is one of the most important nights of my career. But hey, what could be worse? Going with a loser or solo. In my book, solo wins hands down."

I glanced away, knowing I had said too much. He must think me a pathetic excuse of a woman.

"When is the banquet?" Adam pulled out his cell, swiped it several times and then glanced up at me.

Puzzled, I answered, "December tenth. Why?"

My thoughts rolled back to Jeremy and his duplicity. Or does one call it *quadplicity*? I didn't want to get back on that dating horse again. Thinking about dating any man turned my stomach.

"I own a tux and black tie and I'm available." He waited for my response.

Shocked to my core, I wondered why this guy, a virtual stranger, was willing to do a favor for me. Oh, yeah, he was my next-door neighbor, but like I said, we weren't friends or even good acquaintances.

"You're the first. I've never met a man who owns his own tux besides my boss."

"It comes in handy"—his voice softened—"like now."

"Yeah, but mention a fundraiser and most men will turn and run without giving it another thought."

Is he a paid escort? I thought better of him, yet I knew nothing about Adam. "What exactly do you do that you would own your own tux?"

His two adorable dimples appeared as he cocked a brow. He had probably read my thoughts.

"I'm in investments. And the tux? There are times I have to attend black tie functions. It's handier to have my own."

A little vague, but at least being in investments proved he wasn't a gigolo.

"Then you realize these things can be very boring."

"Yes, but I've been to a few fundraisers in my career. If the food's good ..." He shrugged.

"Just like a guy, always thinking of his stomach."

"Hey, I'm at least honest. That's gotta count for something."

"That's true." I liked this guy.

"I sampled the food before choosing the caterer. The food was delicious." I made a grimace. "Still I hate to ask you to sacrifice yourself on the banquet altar."

"You aren't. I'm volunteering."

"And you're not afraid you'll have to snub me later in the hall or when we pass in the stairwell to avoid becoming my permanent bailer?"

"Permanent bailer?" His brow wrinkled.

"Yeah. You know, ask you to bail me out again for some cause of equal or more boring distinction."

He shook his head. "That would never happen. I know how to say *no*. But ..."

"Ah-h-h. The *but* hammer."

Adam's eyes sparkled as he studied me for several uncomfortable seconds. I knew it was too good to be true. He was going to retract his offer.

"No. I'm not backing out. But to ease your conscience about me volunteering as your plus-one, how 'bout we make a trade?"

What was I getting into? He had the look of a man who knew how to barter and come out on top.

"Trade? Trade what?" I gave him a suspicious glance, pulling my jacket up tight around me to help ward off the chill but more to ward off the feeling of my own vulnerability. I really didn't know this guy from Adam— *ha-ha funny, Whitney*—and now he wants to trade favors. What if he was some kind of pervert or serial killer?

"What kind of trade?" This time, I studied him.

He gave a short laugh. "Oh, nothing as nefarious as your mind is conjuring up."

"I wasn't …" *Busted.*

Rolling his eyes, he waved me off.

"Like you, I find myself in a similar situation for my company Christmas party." His gaze returned to his cellphone. "We could exchange services. You know, I help you. You help me. That way, you won't feel so bad about me offering my services."

I was beginning to like this guy more and more … as a quasi-friend, that is.

"I find it hard to believe that you don't have a little black book just chuck full of names of desirable women who would be more than willing to say yes if you asked."

Why was I being snarky when he was offering a solution?

Squirming beneath his gaze, I said, "I'm sorry, that came out all wrong. It's just, I-ah-I figured a guy as good-looking as you would have any number of women lining up for the pleasure of your company." There I go again. Why couldn't I stop my tongue from running off?

I swallowed. "I'm sorry. I just washed my mouth and now it seems I can't do a thing with it. I'll shut up now." I glanced off, clamping my lips together.

His hardy laughter did wonders for easing my humiliation.

"I guess I should say thank you for the compliment. However, concerning my *little black book*"—he paused— "there are plenty of names, but no one I care to call. And what about you? I would think any number of men would be more than happy to accompany you. Hmm?"

There was that raised brow again.

"Here we are, both in need of a stand-in, and one of us is making excuses." He tilted his head in my direction. "I'm really not a bad fellow once you get to know me."

"No it's not you …"

"Well, that's good to know. The way I see it, my suggestion is a win-win solution."

"Since you put it that way … I accept. But first I need to see if my schedule is free for your event. What date is your party?"

I pulled my cellphone from my pocket, thumbed through the calendar, then glanced his direction.

His deliberate gaze caused my insides to clinch. I couldn't read his thoughts. Now I wished I'd stayed inside or at the very least given him a firm *no thanks*.

"December sixteenth."

Pulling my bottom lip through my teeth, I scanned the date. "I have an office party at work that afternoon." To refuse his generous offer now would seem rude. "However, if your party doesn't start too early, I believe I could manage to duck out of mine in time to go with you."

"Unlike yours, mine isn't a black tie affair, but it is a dressy event that starts at seven. As long as we leave here by 6:30, we can make it in plenty of time. But if we're a few minutes late, no matter."

"That shouldn't present a problem." I knew if I prepared everything ahead of time, I could scramble home, shower, and get dressed in less than an hour, doable ... barely. *Was I really thinking about doing this? ... Yes.* "I accept."

Once we were done exchanging information, I decided I should go back inside. I didn't want Adam to think I had expectations of us becoming bosom buddies or anything additional. After all, we were only going to be stand-ins for the holidays, nothing more. After that, we would go back to *Hi. Have a nice day* ... in the hallway again.

With my feet firmly planted on the ground, I said, "Adam, thank you for volunteering. I sincerely appreciate your offer to help. I'll see you on the tenth, if not before."

"You're welcome. I believe this will be the beginning of a solid friendship. Who knows, I may need to borrow a cup of sugar one day. Now I know who to borrow it from ... my friend, Whitney, next door." His smile nearly melted my insides, turning me into a puddle on my balcony.

"Sure, anytime. Thanks again, and goodnight." I moved inside, closed the glass patio door, shutting out the night and my strange encounter.

"Calm down, oh beating heart. It's only a plus-one exchange. The man is out of your league.

I prepared a cup of hot chocolate while I milled over the two events Adam and I would attend together. He certainly was the stuff of a woman's dreams, but I knew better than to remotely think of him in that way.

Deep inside, I knew Adam wasn't a man to be dismissed lightly. I also knew if I wasn't careful, Adam could become *too* important, which would never do.

Now, how does one go about keeping a relationship on a friendly, even plane with an attractive, desirable man?

19

Chapter 2

The obnoxious noise dragged me out of my delightful dream. I couldn't remember what the dream was, but I knew it was delightful because I was smiling. At least I was right up to the moment I rolled over to slap my alarm.

The infernal buzzing didn't stop. I realized the loathsome racket wasn't coming from my clock but from my cellphone.

If it was Mom or another member of my family, I was going to let them have it for waking me at such an ungodly hour. Saturdays were sacred and the only day I allowed myself to sleep in.

Shoving the hair from my face, I rolled over, grabbed the irritating phone, and swiped my finger across the screen.

"Hel-hello?" I cleared the frog from my throat while waiting for a response.

"Hi, Whitney?" The male caller didn't sound sure.

The cobwebs in my head were blown out by the gale force wind brought about by Adam's voice. It affectively wiped my brain clean of all rational thought.

Wide-awake and tingling, I scooted up in bed, propping my back against the headboard. "Adam?"

The adrenaline caused by his laughter zipped through me like a double shot of espresso.

"Yes, sleepyhead, it's Adam. And I see I woke you. Sorry."

Even if we were the very best of friends, I don't believe I could ever get used to his deep, sexy voice. Which at the moment was playing havoc with my early morning emotions that were bouncing all over the place.

"I apologize for waking you. Go back to sleep. I'll hang up and call you later."

"No. No, that's fine." I swiped a hand across my crust-laden eyes. "Once I'm awake, I find it's impossible to go back to sleep."

"My fault entirely."

"Don't worry about it. Did you need something?"

My mind was racing a mile a minute. With a quick glance at the clock, I saw it was barely seven a.m. What could my hunk of a next-door neighbor want at this hour? Back out of our agreement? If so, he could have done it later in the day. Maybe it was for the best this way.

"I was wondering if you'd be up to a brisk walk to Mickey's for breakfast. And since I woke you, my treat."

"I can buy my own."

"I know you can, but it's the least I could do for calling so early."

What was up with this guy? First volunteering as my stand-in date and now breakfast. *Moving way too fast.*

"I have a proposition I'd like to discuss that I think would be mutually beneficial to both of us. What do you say? Can you be ready in twenty minutes?"

"That doesn't give me enough time to shower."

"No need to shower. Put on your warm-ups and jogging shoes and tie your hair up in that cute little ponytail you wear. I'll meet you in the hall in twenty."

"I can't ..." I was speaking to thin air. He'd already hung up. The man was a bit arrogant to presume he could snap his fingers and I'd jump to do his bidding.

My head of steam dissolved when I realized what Adam had said. He had noticed me in my warm-ups and ponytail. I wasn't sure if I should be flattered or appalled. Had he meant it as a compliment or a joke?

It didn't matter. He asked for it. And since he did, he was going to get me in my full workout regalia, ponytail and all.

Maybe this stand-in bargain wasn't such a good idea after all. Adam sure liked to dictate and expected me to hop when he called. Well, maybe I'll just let him cool his heels in the hall for a while. I wasn't going to rush for any man, including Adam Ryder.

By seven-eighteen, I was in the hall waiting on Mr. Dictator himself.

Hair in ponytail, headband over my ears, wearing warm-ups and tennis shoes, with a dash of makeup ... Hey, I couldn't let him see me worse for wear even if it was his suggestion.

With a smidgen of irritation, I lifted my hand to pound on his door. The door opened before my fist touched the wood. Out walked Adam with a sparkle in his eyes.

"I like a woman who's prompt. And, I might add, you look beautiful this morning."

His warm smile and compliment knocked the bluster out of my temper. The man seemed to know his way around women and what to say at just the right time. I'd have to keep on my toes around him.

"You don't look half-bad yourself." *Now where did that come from?*

"Half-bad?" Playfully wrinkling his brow, his adorable dimples showed up. Thanks … I think." He motioned toward the stair exit. "Shall we?"

Apparently, he meant for this to be a real workout.

Though we lived on the twelfth floor of the building, I often took the stairwell to keep in shape. Many times, I passed Adam coming up on my way down or vice-versa, so he knew the stairs were nothing for me.

Neither of us said much on our brisk walk except for general chatter. He asked me about my work, and surprisingly, he listened with interest. Or it could be that he was very good at disguising his boredom.

Since I knew he was an investor but not much more, I asked him about his job.

"Not much to tell. Boring stuff."

"Couldn't be any more boring than mine. But I do like where I work."

"I could tell the way you light up when you talk about it. Your work with charitable foundations speaks well for you."

"Thank you." His compliment thrilled me.

He glanced up at the sky and then at me. "I like where I work, but it's not as big-hearted as yours. I buy and sell companies. I search out struggling businesses—see if we can shore them up and make them profitable again. In doing so, sometimes we make enemies."

"How so?"

"If we see the company is struggling due to poor management, most times we change out the whole workforce, start off with a clean slate. Often we're able to turn them around. But if not, we put them back on the market."

"I would hate to be in your position having to lay off people."

"It's my least favorite part. But I don't personally have to fire the employees. There are others that take care of

23

that. Like I said, my job's nothing as benevolent as what you do." He fell silent, introspective.

When we reached Mickey's, instead of waiting at the back of the line, Adam walked past everyone straight to the hostess. She smiled, said something to him, and then handed him two menus.

Standing back at the door behind a long line of people, my mouth gaped open at his audacity.

He glanced around and then looked at me and motioned.

I turned to look behind me then realized he was signaling for me to follow him.

As I passed the glaring, hungry customers who had been standing in line for a while, I kept up a steady respectful stream of *sorry. Excuse me, please. Sorry.* By their looks and murmurs, I don't believe my piddley words helped much.

Adam led us to a table in the corner with a view of McKinney Avenue. He waited for me to be seated before he sat down.

Chalk one up for Adam. He had nice manners, even if he did cut to the front of the line.

The place was eclectic with quaint little tables and chairs that didn't match. They also offered seating around wrought iron tables in a tented patio area with heat. The mixture of smells floating through the air caused my stomach to clinch with anticipation.

When I looked up from the menu, Adam, a silly grin in place, was watching me intently. I wondered if a big fat zit had taken that moment to reveal itself. Or maybe my hair was sticking out at odd angles.

"Something wrong?" I touched my hair to smooth it down.

"No."

Oh, great! Now he chooses to be the monosyllabic-answer-man.

Needing to fill the awkward silence, I asked, "Have you already decided?"

Duh. Foregone conclusion with his menu closed.

"I'm having my usual."

"Which is?"

"Mickey's omelet."

"Sounds good." I stared at him with a suspicious glint. "*Hmm.* Immediate seating. Familiar with the menu. My amateur Sherlock Holmes instinct tells me you come here often."

"Often enough."

"This is my first." I glanced around wondering why I hadn't tried this place before now.

"Anything you order will be great."

"I'll take your word for it." I scanned the menu and found choosing from all the mouth-watering selections was difficult. I wanted to order a little bit of everything but knew that was insane, not to mention Adam would think he had a porker on his hands.

After placing our order, I began to feel self-conscious again. I had no idea why Adam wanted to meet for breakfast, and he didn't seem anxious to alleviate my curiosity. Yet, his earlier *I have a proposition* worried my mind.

Proposition could mean a lot of things to different people. The problem was I didn't know what proposition meant to Adam.

"You mentioned a proposal?" I shied away from the word *proposition*. I wasn't gonna get caught in that trap.

He nodded, unconsciously lining up his tableware and then glanced up.

Before now, I hadn't realized just how incredibly blue his eyes were, especially set against the backdrop of his olive skin and framed by thick, black lashes—lashes that would make most women envious, including me. However, sitting across from him with the light shining through the window, I received my first full impact, or I should say jolt.

"After you went inside last night, I got to thinking."

I pulled my mind away from the remarkable eyes and tried to make sense of what Adam was saying.

"Besides the Christmas parties, I have several other holiday functions where I could use a date. It would make life easier not to have to ask someone else. I'd be more than willing to exchange favors with you. What do you think?"

"What do you have in mind?" Coming from Adam out of the blue, I wasn't prepared to give an answer until I knew exactly what his offer entailed.

"Well for starters, I have this family Thanksgiving function. It would just go easier for me if I brought a date. And at the moment, like you, I don't have anyone to ask who wouldn't read more into the family gathering than intended. I believe you understand my meaning."

"I do." I nodded, fully aware he was laying down ground rules for our friendly arrangement, emphasis on *friendly*—as in temporary, *no strings attached.*

"I'm sorry, but my family is expecting me home for Thanksgiving. So, going with you is out of the question."

"Does your family live in Dallas?"

"Yes." This guy was a real puzzle, one I felt sure I wouldn't figure out in this lifetime.

"Is your Thanksgiving Thursday or Saturday?"

"Thursday. Why?" Shifting from hellos one minute to bosom buds and stand-in companions the next. What guy did that, especially one who looked as good as Adam?

A smile crept across his face. "Then it'll work."

"What'll work?" Had I lost something in the translation?

"Thanksgiving. Our dinner always takes place on Saturday. Every year, my family has a holiday starter bash the Saturday after Thanksgiving to usher in Christmas. If you'd like, I could accompany you to your family gathering, and then you accompany me on Saturday." He raised his brows. "What do you say?"

He waited patiently without trying to persuade me while I thought through the pros and cons. His worth as a man climbed a few notches higher in my estimation for being patient.

Knowing my family wasn't expecting me to bring home a date for Thanksgiving dinner, I really didn't need to have Adam accompany me. But since he so willingly came to my rescue, I felt I should oblige him.

"I'll go with you, but you don't need to come on Thursday. They aren't expecting me to bring anyone."

"More the better? I'll be your surprise."

"Oh, that's not necessary." I shook my head, not sure I wanted to have to explain Adam to my family.

"I'd like to come along, unless it'll make it awkward for you and them."

There was the odd chance Adam's presence would stop everyone from asking the *when* questions—*when are you going to find a man. When are you going to get married? When are you going to start a family? When, when, when …*

And on the other hand, the family dinner would give me a chance to see how Adam conducted himself around strangers. A trial run of sorts might not be such a bad idea.

If things didn't work out—like if he was obnoxious or didn't know how to handle himself—I would keep my end of the bargain. I would accompany him to his family dinner, then tell him our arrangement wasn't working and I wouldn't need him to attend my Christmas banquet.

"All right. Thanksgiving dinner will be a good trial run for both of us. I'll tell Mom I'm bringing a friend. Of course, everyone will draw their own conclusions since I rarely bring home a male friend. So, be prepared to be bombarded with questions."

27

"I can handle questions as long as *we* know what's what." He cocked his brow.

Stiffening, I said, "You are perfectly safe with me. I don't have time, nor am I looking for a serious relationship. I can't afford to have any distractions."

"Great. Then it's settled." Adam leaned back in his chair, apparently satisfied with our negotiations. He pulled out his cellphone. "Why don't we check our calendars for other events where we may need a partner? That way, we'll have everything booked for the season through New Years. How does that sound?"

"All right. Except, I'd like to add if we find for any reason we want to cancel our agreement … no harm, no foul. Ok?"

"I agree." He began going through his iPhone calendar, seemingly unconcerned.

I did the same. Before the food came, we had down each other's calendar events, which fortunately, except for two, didn't conflict. We agreed we'd go early to one of them and arrive late to the other, that way both events would be covered.

We chatted between bites. Adam seemed genuinely interested in what I had to offer. Though we had many things in common, to say we were compatible might be stretching it a bit.

It would be easy to fall for a guy like him. He had a lot going for him, and not just in the looks department.

I shook my mind mentally. Going down that road would only lead to disaster. Problems were something I didn't need, especially since we were next-door neighbors. And, I didn't want to be looking for a new place to live.

Chapter 3

Sandy Lakeland, the pastor's wife, caught my hand and pulled me aside the moment I walked into the church vestibule. The woman was my mother's age, with small wrinkles beginning to form at the corner of her brown eyes. I hoped I looked as good as she did when I reached her age.

"Whitney, honey, I've been looking for you. I was afraid you wouldn't be here this morning." Her smile was warm, inviting, and meant ... *I have something I need you to do.*

I don't have time for this, especially now during the holidays.

"I know you are terribly busy with work and all, but I had no one else to call who could do the job and do it as efficiently as you."

Standing there patiently, I waited for the ax to drop and cut to the core of the problem. There's no denying my attitude stank. I'd be the first to admit it. However, at the moment my proverbial plate of goodwill was already full to running over. I didn't need to add one more thing to the heaped up chaotic pile that consisted of my life and any free time I might have left.

Be firm. Say, sorry, I wish I could help, but I can't. Then walk away. "Sandy, this isn't—"

"I wasn't sure if you heard, Kathy Felder's mom is in the hospital in critical condition. She flew to Ohio to be with her yesterday afternoon."

"I'm so sorry. I'll keep them in my prayers."

She patted my hand. "I know you will, dear. I wouldn't expect anything less from you. And though we will miss her dearly, this emergency has left us in a bind. We are at the moment without a director for the children's pageant."

Sandy gave me a sad, piteous look. My stomach plummeted.

"I assured Kathy that I would find someone suitable to take over. That's when you came to mind."

Of course it was. I should have checked my stinky attitude at the door. "I'm afraid—"

"Before you say no." She raised her hand to stop my refusal. "Please consider what this would mean to the children, not to mention, it would take a load off Kathy's mind." Her smile was pleasant with a hint of regret. "Kathy suggested you would be perfect for the job. Everyone still talks about the wonderful children's pageant you handled a few years back."

"Sandra, with my job responsibilities, I don't see how—"

"You're our only hope, dear." Patting my arm, she gave me a pleading look. "Unfortunately, no one else has your ability with music and also able to follow through and give us a brilliant children's pageant." Her smile turned warm and affectionate. "Did your mother happen to mention your niece Mandy is one of the angels? She's such a little darling."

Oh, great! She's bringing out the big torpedo.

I knew I was had, the moment she mentioned Mandy. Mom and the others would never let me live in peace if I refused.

Why hadn't I stayed home this morning? I took a deep breath to give her a firm *no*. My conscience bombarded me with guilt from all the years Mom and Dad drilled into us kids that we were to serve even if it hurt. And believe me, it was hurting.

Two little arms wrapped around my legs, affectively cutting off my refusal.

"Auntie Whitty."

Though four years old, my niece still wasn't able to pronounce Whitney, but I loved her to pieces. She was my pride and joy.

"Mama said you're my teacher for the Trismas play."

Before I bent down on eye level for a real hug from my niece, I saw the confident smile on Sandra's face. She knew she had her stand-in director for the children's pageant.

"You better give me a proper hug, little missy."

Mandy squeezed my neck tight enough to cut off circulation and then as a grand finale, gave me one huge, wet kiss on my cheek.

"I'm gonna be an angel wif a long white robe. I get to wear a halo on my head too." She twisted back and forth.

"You will make a beautiful angel."

"I know. That's what Nana said." Mandy bobbed her head up and down, her little flaxen curls bouncing.

Clasping Mandy's hand, I said, "Let me finish talking with Mrs. Lakeland, then you can tell me all about it."

Still wishing I could say no, I stood and looked at Sandra. "I guess you have your substitute director."

"Wonderful."

"However … if Kathy gets back in time, I will step down and she will take over."

"Why, of course, dear." Sandra's gaze strayed to a couple entering the church as she patted my shoulder again. "All of Kathy's things for the play are in the cabinet in the youth hall. I'll give you a call tomorrow."

31

Off she flittered like a butterfly to another unsuspecting flower.

Mandy tugged on my hand. "Can I sit wif you?"

"Yes, if your mama says it's OK."

A little frown appeared but vanished when she saw Jenny, one of her little friends. The child was standing beside her mother who was talking with my sister, Shelly. Mandy dropped my hand, ran over to Jenny, and started chattering away.

I followed but stood to one side while I waited for my sister to finish.

"No," She glanced down at Mandy. "Zack wasn't able to get leave. But we hope he'll be back by Mandy's birthday in April."

We had all known it was a long shot for Zack to make it back in time for Christmas when his elite reconnaissance squad was called up for duty. Apparently, we had our answer. It would be months before he'd make it home.

Shelly ran her hand over her beautiful baby bump. The reminder brought home Zack wouldn't be here for the baby's birth either. The baby was due the second week in January.

I made a mental note to set aside time to spend with Shelly and my niece, especially as we approached the holidays.

I felt terrible I had almost turned Sandra down. Giving my time was small in comparison to what Zack was giving for our country. The least I could do was to give my niece a little extra happiness, especially now that her father wouldn't be home.

Shelly and I hugged. She gave me a knowing look. "You did said yes to Sandra, right?"

Rolling my eyes, I said. "When has anyone ever turned down a request from that woman." I touched Mandy's shiny curls. "How could I refuse? Especially, when my niece is going to be an angel."

Raising her brow, Shelly smiled, her hands resting across the top of her belly.

"However, unless you have that baby early, I'm going to need your help."

"Since this little fellow doesn't seem to be in any hurry to make his entrance into the world, I should be able to lend you a hand."

"Good. What do you hear from Zack?"

"Only that he'll not be able to make it home for Christmas. He misses us terribly. And he's really getting sick of being away from his family."

"Maybe, he'll opt out after this tour."

Shelly shrugged, a resigned look in her eyes. "It would be nice, but I'm beginning to think things would be too tame for him if he ever left the service."

"Don't worry. When Zack makes the choice to retire, he will find something to give him purpose and meaning, like his little family."

"I hope so."

The music began playing through the speakers, a reminder for everyone to come into the sanctuary and find a seat.

"Shall we?" Shelly motioned toward the doors.

Our little party of three and three-quarters filed down the aisle and found seats halfway. Grace Fellowship wasn't a huge mega-church, but was a nice enough size to know the people who attended on a regular basis and to recognize when we had visitors.

Settling Mandy between us, I took the opportunity to glance around the sanctuary. To my far left and closer to the front, sat Lori Morgan. She was laughing and talking with a man sitting next to her. When the man looked forward, I got the odd feeling I knew him. Then it hit me. Lori's friend closely resembled my next-door neighbor, Adam.

Lori saw me and waved.

I waved back, smiling.

She said something to the man causing him to turn and look.

It *was* Adam. He looked at me oddly before turning back to Lori again.

The heat of embarrassment hit. I barely knew the man, yet we had struck a bargain of sorts, or at least that's what I thought, and now he was here with Lori. Would he be backing out now, or should I?

Fortunately, I lowered my head before Adam could turn to witness the brilliant red in my cheeks flashing like a neon sign. I began digging in my purse hoping my blush would dissipate before anyone noticed.

I felt Shelly's hand on my arm.

"What's wrong?" Her brows were knit together.

Too late. She knew me too well. "Nothing." I didn't look at her, just kept digging.

"You sure?"

"Yes." The word came out agitated. "I'm looking for my lip-gloss. It's in here somewhere." I continued to dig in earnest now with a cause in mind.

"Can I have thum lip gloth too?" Mandy looked at me expectantly.

"Sure, sweetie, if I can find it."

"And not being able to find your lip gloss has caused that beautiful shade of pink in your cheeks?"

I pursed my lips while rolling my eyes at her, still ducking my head.

What could I say? Tell my sister I made a bargain with my neighbor, a practical stranger, because he felt sorry for me. *And that, Sis, is how I got my date for the banquet.* How could I know he was already interested in one of the young women in our church—a new member, no less?

Had he mentioned me to Lori?

Fortunately, the music minister picked that moment to start the service.

"Sorry, sweetie." I looked at my niece. "I must have left it home. Here, let me hold you so you can see up front."

Lifting Mandy, I placed her in my arms as a barrier between Adam and me, just in case he looked my way, which he probably wouldn't.

We began singing, but my heart wasn't in it. Normally, worship always lifted my spirit. And most Sundays I would have been up front with the backup singers, but my work had prevented me from practicing with the group last Thursday for today's service. Thankfully, it had, or I would have been standing on the platform facing Lori and Adam with no one to shield me from his gaze.

From time to time, I took quick, secret glances in Adam's direction.

I didn't know why I felt so bad. Maybe because he hadn't mentioned he was dating Lori. And now that I knew the other woman, well, I'm just saying, it felt awkward.

Way to go, Whitney. Steal another woman's man.

Maybe, if I'd known Lori better, I would have known Adam and she were friends … close friends, as it seemed.

How could I have known though? Lori had just started attending our church a few months ago, but this was the first time I'd ever seen her with a man. And now, I was virtually dating *her* guy—well actually, not dating. Ours was a stand-in date situation. How to explain it to her if Adam hadn't?

When the music portion of the service was over, and as we were being seated, I happened to glance in Adam's direction. He gave me a nod and smiled. I nodded briefly before looking away.

Again, Shelly gave me that curious look of *what's going on?* She glanced in the direction of Lori and Adam, but thankfully they had taken their seats.

Once again, I ignored her.

To say I heard much of Pastor Steve's sermon would be a stretch. However, one particular verse did stick with me, making me feel worse than I already did.

Do unto others, as you would have them do unto you.

I was ready to run forward and confess all, but then remembered, I had nothing to confess.

Adam came up with the plan to exchange favors. He said he didn't have anyone to invite to his holiday functions. How was I to know?

It didn't matter whether Adam and Lori were just friends or something more. Lori would be told about the agreement first chance I got. I didn't want her thinking I had designs on Adam, because I didn't. He wasn't my type. *Well, maybe a little.*

The moment the service was over and the pastor dismissed, I turned to Shelly. "Listen, I hate to rush out, but I forgot my change of clothes. I'll meet you at Mom and Dad's. See you later."

As I moved out into the aisle, I heard my sister and little Mandy calling my name. I ignored them both. I didn't want to explain and take the chance of running into Lori and Adam. My guilt was too heavy to face the *other* woman, at least right now. I'd been on the receiving end and knew how it felt.

I was probably blowing the whole situation out of proportion. But it didn't stop me from rushing out the door of the church to my car. Maybe he did have a plausible explanation, yet I couldn't think of one.

As I drove by the front of the church, I saw Adam take Lori's arm and tuck it inside his as they walked down the steps. They were smiling and talking. They looked like a happy couple. They seemed to love one another. And I had a sinking sensation I was now the other woman.

So why did he say he didn't have anyone he cared to ask? Maybe, they'd had a lover's spat and made up. Or, since we were neighbors, maybe he thought to have a little action on the side.

Well, buster, you've got another think coming. I'm not that kind of a woman.

Chapter 4

If I could, I would have missed Sunday family dinner all together. Not that I didn't like spending time with my folks, I did. It was just that I knew what Shelly would do the minute I stepped inside the house—grill me until she got what she wanted. Information.

Information was something I didn't want to give, especially with everyone present and when I didn't have answers.

If my brother Seth got wind of what I had agreed to, he'd take matters into his own hands. He wouldn't let it happen without a thorough investigation of Adam. In fact, he would probably go to Adam's apartment, grill him until he knew everything there was to know about the guy, even down to what color underwear he wore, … and why that would matter, I don't know. Once Seth gathered all his Intel he'd probably tell Adam under no uncertain terms … *you better back off, buster.*

Being a police detective, Seth had a very suspicious mind. At least it seemed that way when it came to the men I dated. He was way too protective of me, his little sister, which often caused me problems.

Once again, it seemed I had made a big mess without trying. How did I get myself into these scrapes?

I pulled into my parents' drive, stopped the engine, then sat there wishing I didn't have to go inside. Groaning, I pulled the key out of the ignition, not ready to meet the inquisition. Yet, putting it off wouldn't make it easier.

As I reached for the door handle, the thing was snatched from my fingers causing me to yelp. I glared up at my hulk of a brother laughing his head off.

"You moron, you scared the tar out of me." I slid out of the car and glared at him.

He pulled me into a bear hug, lifted me off my feet, and then began turning circles.

Laughing and screaming, I yelled, "Put me down, you big lug, before we both fall down."

Lowering me to the ground, he slapped his hands over his chest. "Ah, you sure know how to hurt a guy who loves you."

Smiling, I grabbed his arm and started toward the house. "Hi to you too, and I love you regardless if you never grow up."

"You can't help but love me." Seth looked down at me in that curious way he had of analyzing everyone. "What's up?" He was a wonderful brother, but at times, like now, he was too astute.

"What makes you think something's up?"

Cocking a brow, he gave me that *you're not fooling me* look.

I glanced straight ahead. "Nothing. Just work. And this time of year everything's more hectic."

"Hmm. Sooner or later, you'll tell me." Seth opened the front door and allowed me to go in first.

"Something smells good. What are we having for dinner? I'm starved." My words were for diverting his attention.

39

"My favorite. Meatloaf, mashed potatoes, green beans, and fried okra."

"Sounds wonderful." I moved into the family room where Dad was watching a football game. "Hey, handsome." I bent and placed a kiss on his cheek.

He barely glanced up from the game. "Hey, yourself. What happened to you? You didn't wait around after church to say hi."

"Sorry, but I wanted to change my clothes before I came over and I didn't want to make dinner late for everyone." Even to my ears it sounded like a lame excuse.

Dad's attention was already on the game again along with Seth's.

I wandered into the kitchen.

"Hi Mom." I gave her a hug and a peck on the cheek. "What can I do to help?"

She smiled and motioned to the steaming bowls lined up on the counter. "Put those on the table. We were just waiting on you to arrive."

Picking up two of the bowls, I carried them to the dining room table before going back for the others. My stomach rumbled.

Shelly passed me with glasses of tea in her hands. Thankfully, she was too busy to interrogate. But I knew it was only a matter of time before she'd ferret out what was going on.

Mandy stood to the side, her bottom lip sticking out.

I bent down eye-level with her. "What's a matter, sweetie?"

"You didn't let me ride wif you."

"I'm *sooo* sorry. But for sure next time."

"Ok. Don't forget." She brightened up and skipped around the room.

"Let's all sit down and pray before the food gets cold." Mom bustled into the room, a basket of hot rolls in her hands, motioning everyone to their places.

After Dad said the blessing, Seth grabbed the platter in front of him, shoveled off a hefty portion of meatloaf and then passed it on.

"What happened at church this morning?" Shelly handed me the potatoes.

The food passing was suspended and everyone turned to look at me.

"What do you mean *what happened?*" Seth jumped on Shelly's choice of words like a gnat on a juicy peach.

"Nothing happened." I tried for nonchalance, but by the look of everyone I hadn't pulled it off. "If you're through with those green beans, I would like some, please."

Seth narrowed his eyes, took another spoonful, and then passed the bowl.

"Don't give me that. You fled the church like the building was on fire." Shelly gave me a beady-eyed stare, as if to say *you will come clean.*

"Hardly."

Again *that* look.

"Well, if you must know, I saw someone I didn't want to talk to. I thought the best way to avoid them was to leave first."

"Oh, honey."

Mom's wagging head and look of disappointment had me squirming inside.

"We've taught you better than that. If someone's wronged you, you're to show them love and compassion, forgiving them."

"It wasn't anything like that. I just didn't want to get stuck talking. I'll get in touch with them later today." Thinking to change the subject, I said, "Did you know Kathy Felder's mom is in the hospital in critical condition?"

"Yes, we've been praying for both of them. You will be taking over the pageant?" My mother's question was more a foregone conclusion.

41

"I told Sandra I would. However, I wish she had found someone else. My schedule is really tight, especially now. I won't have as much time to devote to the play."

"I'm going to be the best angel ever." Mandy beamed up at me.

"Thanks, I knew I could count on you." Seeing her smile bolstered my spirit.

"I may be calling on you and Shelly to help on the costumes."

Mom slathered butter across her roll. "I'll be more than happy to help. Just let me know when and what."

"I'll do what I can." Shelly ran her hand over her rounded belly. "Just as long as this baby doesn't decide to come early."

"He better stay put, at least until after the children's play." I slid a slice of meatloaf onto my plate.

The conversation moved around the table from one thing to the next. I was grateful it didn't revolve back around to me. I didn't want to tell them about Adam and Lori, not until I knew the facts.

One thing for sure, as soon as I could, I would ask Adam about Lori. If they were an item, then the deal was off.

Chapter 5

My insides were in knots. I disliked confrontation more than most. In fact, I tried to avoid conflict of any kind whenever possible. Mama always called me the little peacemaker. Probably why my job appealed to me. I like to do whatever I can to help others and resolve issues. But the matter of Lori and Adam wasn't something I could let slide. Especially, if Lori wasn't aware of the agreement between Adam and me, regardless how innocent.

Thanksgiving was Thursday and my banquet was two weeks after.

My hand shook slightly when I knocked on Adam's door. Down deep I hoped he wasn't home.

Just my luck, he was.

Seeing him caused a knee-jerk reaction. With one welcoming glance, my resolve turned to mush. The fresh woodsy smell I had learned to associate with him, filtered out into the hall.

I couldn't allow the fact he looked and smelled so good deter me from my goal.

"Hi. I think we have a few things to discuss." *Mainly Lori.*

His smile nearly bowled me over. Not even one of Jeremy's smiles could elicit such a response from me, and Jeremy was a lady's man who knew how to turn on the charm.

"What's that saying about great minds? I was just on my way to see you." He moved back into his entry and motioned me inside. "Please, come in."

His floor plan was larger than mine. It was tastefully furnished with traditional furniture, paintings on the walls, and a huge oriental rug on the floor worth a fortune. I wondered if he decorated the place himself or if he'd had help. More than likely one of his lady friends stepped up to do the honors. *Now that was catty.*

"Have a seat."

Picking a chair, I perched on the edge and felt out of my element, which was unusual for me.

"I wasn't aware you attended Grace Fellowship. Lori and I tried to work our way around to where you were sitting, but you were already gone by the time we got there."

Without knowing what game he was playing, I said, "Yes, my family and I have attended the church for a number of years. But I've never seen you there before."

"This morning was my first time. I normally go to a different church, but Lori has been begging me to go with her. So I finally gave in. I've never been able to say no to her."

The sound in his voice and the fondness in his eyes enforced my belief that he had tender feelings for Lori, maybe even love.

Why would he jeopardize their relationship?

Perhaps he talked with her, told her it was too late to back out on me. Maybe that's why she was cool with the arrangement. Still finding it hard to fathom, I needed to know for sure.

"I assume our plus-one arrangement is off now since Lori..." I trailed off, not knowing what to say.

"No. Why would you think that?"

His puzzled look gave me pause. "Well, I just thought maybe she-ah-you would want ..."

"Nothing's changed. Lori knows all about our swap, and she's cool with it. In fact, when I told her, she was in favor of the plan." He looked at me oddly. "Are you wanting to back out?"

"No, I'm not backing out. I just thought-ah-I wanted to make sure she was OK with us? I don't mean us, as in a couple, but that we will be going out together. Well, not technically going out, but ... you know." Flustered, I waved my hands about. My nervousness was not only showing up in my speech but by the heat rising to my cheeks.

"She was surprised but pleased when I told her you lived next door. She thought our arrangement was a good idea."

Maybe Lori and he were just friends, and there wasn't a love attachment after all. But why did I detect a special glimmer in his eyes when he spoke about her?

"Are you having second thoughts?" He studied me.

I felt strangely warm under his scrutiny. It wouldn't be a hard thing to fall for this guy, even though I was still uncertain as to his relationship with Lori.

"Or has Casanova come back around?"

"Casanova?" I felt the little lines between my brows tighten.

"The four-timer." He shrugged indifferently. "Has he come back into the picture?"

"No! That was over six months ago. I wouldn't give him the time of day."

"Good. May I offer you something to drink?" He started toward the kitchen.

"No, I'm fine, thank you."

He turned around, moved to the sofa and sat down facing me.

"If you're sure Lori's ok with this …"

"First off, I don't pass my plans by Lori for her approval." He sounded a little peeved with the subject.

"Well … I thought we should discuss our strategy."

"Strategy? Are we contemplating a war or occupation?" He grinned.

"You haven't met my family. I feel sure it will be a full-fledged frontal attack. They are overly protective and a teensy bit nosey since I'm the baby of the family."

His laughter rumbled through me, leaving a feel-good sensation behind.

"They sound interesting."

The sparkle in his eyes had me wishing I could find someone who was as nice as Adam appeared to be and also had his easy-going mannerisms.

"Oh they're interesting all right. If you'd like, you can skip my families' Thanksgiving. We can pick up Saturday with yours."

"Nope." He shook his head. "I'm not afraid of a little family interrogation."

"If you're sure." I gave him another moment to reconsider.

"Just so there won't be any surprises, I'll give you the short version of what you can expect when you arrive at my parent's home. I come from of a long line of loveable odd ducks."

"Does that mean I need to be on my guard?"

"No. Seth, my unmarried brother, is normal except that he thinks he's God's gift to women, and most women agree. He'll probably bring his latest with him, unless he's in between." I chuckled. "You can expect a thorough once over on your intentions toward me. Just ignore him and don't let him bother you. He thinks no man's good enough for his baby sister. I'll do my best to head him off, but I can't make any promises."

"That bad, huh?"

"You don't know bad until Seth has interrogated you. He's a police detective. Need I say more?"

He raised his brow, his dimples appearing. "Ah, I get the picture. And thanks for the warning. I'd hate to be hauled off in handcuffs."

"Mom and Dad wouldn't let it go that far."

"Any others I should be aware of?"

"Only Amanda."

His brow rose in question.

"Shelly and Zack, my sister and her husband, have a precious but very precocious little four-year-old daughter. Mandy is full of non-stop questions."

"I believe I can handle her."

I just bet you can. Give her one of your smiles, and she'll be in love with you.

"Oh, I almost forgot about Grandmother Bachman. Grams is eighty-nine and has narcolepsy."

"Narcolepsy?"

I nodded my head. "The sleeping disease. I must warn you she is apt to fall asleep and begin snoring without warning. And then there's Aunt Polly, Grams' widowed daughter who lives with her. Come to think of it, I'm going to leave it at that. It might be more interesting to see your response to the rest of my loveable but crazy family."

He looked amused. "I can truly say I'm looking forward to it."

"How about your folks. Anyone you need to warn me about?"

He shrugged. "I don't think you will find my family anywhere near as entertaining as yours. Mine are more ... I wouldn't call them normal exactly. Boring would be a better word."

Without Adam being more forthcoming, I wondered if maybe I had said too much about my adorable but quirky kin. What if I didn't fit in with his? There again, I didn't need to fit in.

The more we were together, the more I found Adam likeable, easy to talk to, and growing on me. Maybe when all was said and done, we would become good friends.

"Would you like to grab a bite to eat?"

I shook my head. "I'm sorry, but I have work to do before tomorrow morning and with this being a short week, I'll be burning the midnight oil. But thanks for the invite. Maybe some other time. I'd best be going." I stood and moved towards the door.

"What time should I pick you up on Thursday?"

I laughed. "If you remember, I live next door, so you don't have to pick me up."

"That's true. So what time are we leaving?"

"How about 11:30. I usually help Mom with preparations. Everyone starts arriving around noon and we eat around one." I hadn't thought the plan through. My mind scrambled for an alternate plan. "So you won't have to sit among strangers, I'll give you the address and you can come in time for dinner. My parents don't live too far from here."

"No, I'd rather we rode together."

"Suit yourself. I hope you like football."

"Sure do."

"Dad will have the games on. My brother and cousins will be there, but like I said, expect a little friendly hazing from that quarter.

"Don't worry. I can hold my own. I don't scare easily."

"Don't say I didn't warn you."

"Duly noted."

I stood. "All right then, I'll see you Thursday, 11:30."

He walked me to his front door then waited in the hall. I felt his gaze on my back all the way to my apartment.

48

When I slid the card over the door card reader, I couldn't keep from glancing back his way.

"Just making sure you get home safely." His eyes were filled with laughter.

Warmth went all through me. I smiled and waved. "I did, and thanks."

Stepping inside, I shut the door, then leaned my back against the cool wood. The web was already weaving its way around my heart.

How in the world would I keep from wanting more than this strictly professional agreement entailed? For sure … I was a goner.

Chapter 6

Since Sunday, I hadn't run into Adam once, which wasn't all that unusual. Before our plan to be stand-ins, weeks, even months, could roll by without seeing him. Then all of the sudden, he'd be there in the hall or stairwell giving me a cheery *hello*.

All week, I found myself looking for Adam, even hoping for a glimpse of him, which was especially unsettling. Not that I wanted to see him, I didn't. Still, at the oddest moments, at work, at home, or while exercising, disconcerting thoughts of him would surface, troubling me.

This arrangement had me reacting totally out of character. No other man had ever affected me like Adam seemed capable of doing. While talking on the phone, I always doodled. Nine times out of ten it would be Adam's name.

Even yesterday when I took the afternoon off to get my hair done I thought of *him*. I asked for a trim and highlights in hopes that the subtle blonde streaks would set off my non-descript mousy-colored hair and maybe give more depth to my brown eyes. One look in the mirror at the finished product had me wishing I'd left my hair alone.

It wasn't that my hair looked awful. It looked great.

However, I didn't want Adam thinking I had changed my appearance to impress him, which I hadn't. *Well,* maybe a little. Come to think of it, I did want to impress him. I wanted him to see me as an attractive and interesting woman.

After all, what woman wouldn't want to look appealing while standing next to a man who looked as if he'd stepped off the cover of GQ Magazine? And, I didn't want him to regret his plus-one choice.

Uptight and nervous, I discarded several outfits before settling on a peach ribbed-knit sweater dress that hugged my figure in all the right places. After adding knee-high brown boots, I took a look in the full-length mirror. On the verge of yanking off the dress and boots, I saw the clock and paused. I had less than ten minutes to freshen my hair and put on lipstick before meeting Adam. This outfit would have to do.

Filled with doubts, I reminded myself I wasn't dressing to impress him anyhow. I finished with several eclectic bangles, a necklace, and earrings. Then after one final look in the mirror, I headed for the door.

I grabbed the plate of fudge off the counter that I'd made the night before, picked up my purse and keys, and then stepped outside my apartment to be greeted by a wolf whistle.

Glancing around, I caught Adam standing outside his apartment watching me, a look of appreciation on his face.

His whistle made my insides light up. His smile, as though he was glad to see me, went a long way to boost my self-confidence. Particularly after Jeremy pointed out that I didn't have enough to hold a man's interest, also the reason why he went looking for several other someones who could.

Wiping my mind of Jeremy's hurtful words, I returned Adam's smile.

"Are you up for a little Singleton family hazing?"

"I have my steel-plate armor on under my shirt." He came toward me, knocking on his chest.

"Oh-ho. Smart fella." There's something to be said about a man's easy-going attitude.

"I believe I can withstand any darts they want to throw."

"They don't use darts, they use bullets." I grinned to let him know I was teasing. "But I'll make sure I stand between you and them if at all possible."

"Talk about emasculating a man." Adam chuckled then sobered. "By the way, you look amazing."

"Why thank you, kind sir." I gave a quasi bow and a cheeky grin, wanting to keep this on a teasing, friendly basis, nothing serious.

"I like what you did to your hair, and that dress ..." He gave me the once over and another wolf whistle. "Let's just say, if we meet any men coming or going, I may have to fight them off."

Feeling my cheeks heat up, I motioned toward the elevator. "Shall we?" I smiled at him. "I might add you cleaned up pretty well yourself."

His brow scrunched together. "Thanks, I believe there was a compliment in there somewhere."

"There was." I punched the button, and the doors to the elevator opened.

Adam placed his hand on the small of my back.

I almost dropped the plate of fudge from the sensation of his touch. I felt hot and a little quivery, much like a schoolgirl on her first date.

"What you got there?"

"Fudge."

"You made it?"

"Of course. I can and do cook."

"Like they say, the proof is in the pudding. In this case, the fudge." He reached under the plastic wrap and filched a piece, tossing it in his mouth."

In a stupor, I watched him chew and swallow the fudge, then averted my eyes before being caught staring.

"No lie. You do cook good, or at least you know how to make fudge."

When he reached for another piece, I slapped his hand and moved the plate out of his grasp. "You can have more at the house."

"You're not fun."

"I've been told that on several occasions."

The doors opened and he guided me with his hand on my back again. This time I was prepared for the warmth his touch provoked, barely. Yet, I figured the imprint of his hand would be seared on my back for some time to come.

"We'll take my car."

"Are you sure?"

"Absolutely. I'm over here."

I presumed it was a macho thing and w*hat the harm*?

Never having seen his car or ridden with Adam before, I wasn't surprised to find he drove a sporty black Audi ragtop. Whenever he took it out on the open road, I felt sure he wouldn't let any dust collect under his wheels.

He proved me right. We made it to my folks' house in record time and without any tickets, even if it was a little dicey at one point.

Adam was just opening my door when my brother drove in behind us.

Seth parked, got out of his Jeep, and then walked in our direction.

Adam grinned when he assisted me out of the car. "If I'm not mistaken, I believe the games have begun." His words were said under his breath as he gave a slight nod in my brother's direction.

"You can leave now if you want." I cocked a comical brow.

"No way. I don't scare off that easily." He took my arm angling us toward the front door. "I'm curious enough to see how this will all play out."

His sparkling gaze seemed to caress my face. For sure, if I weren't careful I would believe those looks were meant for real.

"And another thing, I'm here for the long haul."

Uncertain to his meaning by *the long haul*, I decided to ignore the odd reference.

"Sweet ride." Seth whistled as he gave the Audi the once over. He honed in on Adam. "Hey, Sis, who's your friend?" His cop curiosity was kicking into overdrive. His inquisitive juices were practically drooling down his chin.

"Adam Ryder, this is my brother Seth. Seth this is my neighbor and friend, Adam."

"Neighbor, huh?" He narrowed his gaze. "Friend? What type of friend?"

I smiled sweetly, enjoying the cat enticed by the string game, wondering if Seth would pounce.

For a moment it was pretty touch-'n'-go whether my brother would pull Adam's arms around behind his back to cuff him, or offer him the official good-mannered handshake.

"Welcome. I don't suppose Whitney happened to mention that I'm a police detective?" He gripped Adam's hand like a vice, shaking it and smiling.

"I believe she mentioned something about that." Adam raised a brow, a twinkle in his eyes.

"What do you do for a living?"

"I—"

"Back off Big Brother. Give him a chance to at least get inside the house and sit down before you start grilling him."

Her brother almost looked embarrassed, but ruined it by laughing. "Where are my manners?"

"Gone begging, is where." I shook my head giving Seth an evil eye, which he ignored.

My warnings hadn't been unfounded. Adam was in for some major grilling from my family. And though I would do my best to ease the attack, I couldn't be with him every minute. He'd have to stand on his own for some of the time. I glanced up at Adam and figured he was capable. I just hoped he'd come out unscathed.

Seth grabbed me up into a full bear hug, my feet dangling above the ground. He kissed me on the cheek then released me, latching onto my arm moving smoothly between Adam and me.

"Shall we go inside?"

Ignoring Seth, I stopped and turned, giving Adam a chance to catch up. "Mom and Dad have lived in this house since they were first married."

He came up alongside me, slipping my other arm in his. I felt like the guys were playing tug-of-war and I was the rope. I figured he was showing my brother he could be possessive too, but his touch wasn't the same as Seth's.

His touch made my stomach all fluttery with excitement. And this wasn't even a real date or a real love interest. What would happen if it were?

"Nice place." He looked at the two-story Hill-Country stone house with appreciation.

"Dad built it for Mom as a wedding gift. She won't live anywhere else."

My brother opened the door and motioned for Adam and me to enter first.

Seth winked, quirking a grin in my direction. I was uncertain what he was up to, but whatever it was, I knew I wasn't going to like it.

"Hey, Mom, our little Whitney has brought a fellow home for dinner."

Chapter 7

The house turned silent. Someone even muted the TV, which meant this was a serious business. No one ever dared to interfere with the men watching football.

For some reason, the stillness in the room brought to mind the old child's Christmas poem—*'Twas the night before Christmas ... not a creature was stirring ...* Like statues with inquisitive eyes, everyone's attention was on us.

If I could, I would have grabbed Seth's gun strapped to his ankle and shot him in the foot. Instead, I elbowed him good and hard. "Will you please act your age and behave?"

"No way, Sis. If you're bringing a guy home to meet the folks, then he better be worth it and have a tough enough hide to survive the heat." He purposely stared at Adam.

Adam didn't flinch, just smiled. "I think you'll find my hide is plenty tough. It can withstand sufficient heat and then some."

He bent to whisper in my ear. "You weren't kidding."

His breath next to my skin left me feeling more excited than I should have. This churning of sensations seemed to be happening on a regular basis around Adam.

"There's still time to make a speedy exit." I hoped he wouldn't.

"Not on your life."

At least he wasn't one to take flight at being the brunt of a little friendly hazing.

The silence in the house woke Grandma Bachman from her slumber.

"Is dinner ready?" Her loud question brought about laughter, breaking the Adam trance.

"No, Grams. It'll be at one as usual." Mom stood in the kitchen doorway, assessing Adam.

Shelly stood behind Mom, gawking at us as if we were an abnormality.

"Oh, another hour? In that case, I think I'll have some of those little finger foods. Polly, be a dear and go fetch me a couple of those celery cheese sticks. That should tide me over 'til dinner."

Aunt Polly whispered something in the Grams' ear.

"Who's that you say is with Whitney?" Her loud voice traveled across the room. "I don't think I've seen this one before. He doesn't look like the same fellow who came with her to the last gathering. This one's a whole lot better looking."

Hearing Adam's soft chuckle eased my worries some. At least he was taking everything good-naturedly … even Grams' outburst.

"Whitney, would you like to do the honor of introducing your friend?" Mom jumped in before Grams could say anything more, but it didn't stop Gram's interest still aimed at Adam.

Somehow, I knew Grams would have a few more awkward questions before the day was over.

"Ready or not here we go," I said under my breath, placing a huge smile on my face. "Everyone, this is Adam Ryder. He's a friend and neighbor of mine." I turned to Adam and began the introductions.

I had made it all around the room when my sixteen-year-old cousin, Johnny, popped in from outside.

"Whose wheels?"

"I believe you're talking about Adam's car." I smiled at his youthful enthusiasm.

"Sweet ride." Johnny, full of himself, looked Adam over, then grinned. "I don't suppose you'd let me take your baby out for a spin."

"No, he won't," I said. "Adam, this overconfident teen is my younger cousin, Johnny."

"I'm not all that young." His mouth pinched together.

"Shake hands, son." My Uncle Jerry Don gave Johnny a stern look. "But don't you dare go asking for the keys."

"Nice to meet you, sir." He stuck out his hand toward Adam, then leaned in. "Seriously, if you need someone to blow the soot out of the engine, I'm your man."

"His soot's just fine." I interjected.

Little Mandy chose that moment to burst into the room. "Auntie!" She hugged my legs then looked up at me. "What's soot?"

"It's black gunk." I scooped her up in my arms, receiving a tight squeeze.

"What's his name?" Mandy pointed at my companion.

"Adam."

"Adam like in the Bible?" Her eyes grew round.

"Yes."

She looked around the room then back at Adam. "Where's Eve?"

Muffled chuckles came from my sidekick and the rest of the room.

"There isn't an Eve … yet." Adam's dimples were still in place.

"There is too. My Sunday teacher read me the story."

"That's another man. I'm related to him though." He grinned at Mandy. "What's your name?"

"My name is Amanda Kay Miller. I'm almost five."

Keeping a straight face, Adam leaned in toward my niece. His arm rubbed against mine, causing an earthquake in my stomach.

"You have a pretty name, and you're as pretty as your auntie."

Mandy tucked her head into my shoulder, taking peeks at Adam.

"Adam, welcome to our home." Mom hadn't moved from the doorway of the kitchen. "Any friend of Whitney's is always welcome. I hope you came with an appetite."

"I certainly did."

"Good." She motioned to the buffet table loaded with appetizers. "If you're hungry, please help yourself? Dinner will be ready in about an hour." She turned to me. "Whitney, dear, after you've shown Adam around, I could use your help in the kitchen."

Mandy squirmed to get down. She took one more look at Adam before running off to the playroom. Apparently Adam and Eve no longer mattered.

I said, "You want to follow me?"

We walked through the house. I showed him where the facilities were and where he could escape, if need be. By the time we got back to the family room, I pointed to the overstuffed chair, mysteriously left vacant, next to my dad's recliner. The game was back on full blast, and the men were bemoaning a bad call by one of the referees.

Adam's attention was drawn to the screen as he eased himself down into the chair.

"If it starts getting too rough, come get me. I'll be in the kitchen."

"Sure." Already forgotten, Adam turned to my father. "Who's playing and what's the score?"

Dad rattled off the information and, then gave me a nod. "He'll be fine. You go help your Mom."

Already engrossed in the game, I wasn't certain Adam knew what I had said or that I was even leaving the room. On the other hand, I knew my father wouldn't make Adam feel uncomfortable, nor would he allow the others to quiz him unmercifully.

The moment I entered the kitchen, Shelly was there beside me.

"Okay, give."

"Give what?"

Shelly crossed her arms and let out a huff. "You know perfectly well what."

I gave her a look of absolute indifference. "His name is—"

"I know his name, but what I want to know is, how did you meet? And if I'm not mistaken, wasn't he at church Sunday with that new girl, Lori Morgan?"

"I met Adam at my complex. He's my next door neighbor."

"Hmm, since when did you start dating your neighbor?" Shelly raised her brow.

"We're not dating. We're friends."

Shelly crossed her arms and tapped her foot.

I rolled my eyes unable to ignore her question. "Yes, he did come with Lori on Sunday. I believe they're close friends. She invited him to church." I kicked myself mentally. I hoped they were close friends. However, as far as I knew, they were romantically involved.

"Which is it? You're not sure, or you don't want to know?"

"I don't know. When I asked him to dinner, Adam did say that it wouldn't be a problem with Lori."

My sister had voiced the same questions I'd asked myself numerous times and still had no answers. Only now it sounded a little sordid, even to me too.

I certainly didn't want to make an enemy or hurt Lori's feelings.

On the way home, I planned on asking Adam just how involved they were—friends or more than friends. And if more than friends, then I would bow out of the picture.

"That's enough, Shelly." Mom gave her a stern look. "Right this minute, I need your help and Whitney's too if we're ever going to get this meal on the table by one."

Picking up the peeler, I started on the potatoes. "To ease your mind, Adam and I are just friends, nothing more. He would have spent a lonely day at home. I knew Mom wouldn't mind an extra, so I invited him. Nothing more. End of story."

My sister snorted her disbelief. "He wasn't looking at you like there was nothing more, end of story. That man is interested."

"*Ohhh, pleeeze.* He's a nice, thoughtful guy. Don't read more into the situation than is actually there."

I wished I hadn't invited Adam. He would have been okay with just me attending his affair on Saturday, but no, I couldn't let well enough alone. And one thing for sure, I wasn't about to mention I was going to his folks' for dinner on Saturday.

"Shelly, clean the broccoli and put it in the steamer."

"Well, all I'm saying is, I hope you get to know him better before you become too involved with the man." Shelly yanked the refrigerator open, dug in the crisper, and pulled out a large bag of broccoli.

"We're friends and neighbors, nothing more. Neither of us has any intention otherwise, plain and simple." Tired of the conversation, I turned to Mom. "Boy, am I getting hungry. Everything smells fabulous."

My sister froze and turned red, her gaze behind me.

I turned to see what held her attention.

Adam stood in the doorway watching me, the coffee pot in his hand, his expression unreadable. "I hope I'm not

61

intruding, but I'm afraid I took the last cup." He held out the pot.

"Oh, here. Let me get that." Mom rushed across the kitchen island and grabbed the pot. "You go on back and enjoy the game. There'll be a fresh one in a few minutes."

He looked like he wanted to say something to me, but nodded at my mom instead. "Thanks."

When he left the room, my sister became flustered.

"How much did he hear?" I hoped he'd just walked in, but by the look on Shelly's face he'd been there in time to hear my declaration, and maybe part of my sister's.

"I'm sorry. I don't know. I looked up and he was standing there." She wiped her hands on a dishcloth.

My heart sank. "No matter. Like I said, we don't have any expectations beyond friendship."

"Are you sure?" Shelly's brows knit together.

"Positive."

My sister and her curiosity the size of the whole outdoors had me squirming.

How would I explain to Adam what was being said? Maybe he wouldn't mention the conversation. However, if he did then I'd explain why I said what I did. Surely he couldn't find fault with my reasoning.

Now if I could keep my heart steady and on the right course, my words would remain true. But for some reason, my heart wasn't listening to my head.

Adam Ryder was one appealing man who was becoming more important to me by the minute.

Chapter 8

Dinner went well. No frontal or side attacks. Even Grams somewhat cooperated. She didn't ask many questions or fall asleep at the table. Most of her alertness was due to Adam though.

Like bookends, she sat on one side of Adam and I on the other. The placement made it difficult for me to divert her attention or stop her when she strayed into gray areas, which seemed to be about every time she opened her mouth.

To say Grams was smitten with Adam was putting it mildly. Even when we retired to the family room, she managed to sidle up next to him on the sofa. She continued to look up at him adoringly while keeping him and anyone else who would listen entertained with stories. Most of them about me. She aired all the idiosyncrasies of my juvenile behavior and lack of judgment while growing up.

There were several times I wished I could have told her to put a sock in it and would have, too, if I hadn't been raised to respect my elders. So I clamped my teeth tightly, sealed my lips to the words chomping to come out, and tried to smile. If I hadn't been made of sterner stuff, I would have crawled away and cried in shame. However, Adam seemed thoroughly amused.

Me? I couldn't wait for the evening to end.

I didn't know who would open Pandora's box next and unleash more humiliating details of my childhood and teen fiascoes.

"Whitney, dear, your Christmas presents are in the trunk of my car." Aunt Polly rose from her chair. "Mother and I will be leaving soon. Why don't we go now while we still have a little daylight left? That way you'll be able to pick out your gifts and put them in your car."

"Sure." I glanced over at Adam, who was engrossed in yet another of Gram's tales.

"Why don't you come along, Adam." Aunt Polly, ever the diplomat, smiled at him. "You can help Whitney choose."

"I'd love to." He stood, looking sweetly down at Grams. "If you'll excuse me, duty calls."

Not wanting Adam to be a part of Aunt Polly's yearly ritual, yet, not knowing how to dissuade him without sounding inhospitable, I held out my hand. "If you'll give me your keys, I can put the presents in the car. That way you can stay inside where it's warm."

"If it's all the same, I'd like to go. As it is, I've been sitting too long and need to stretch my legs."

"Great."

The sinking feeling that he might laugh at Aunt Polly's peculiar ritual had me anxious. I wished I had told her I'd come by next week to pick out the gifts, but it was too late now.

We followed her out into the late afternoon. The shadows were long. Dusk was on the verge of taking away what little sun was left, adding a crisp chill to the air. The crunch of leaves beneath our feet served as the backdrop to Aunt Polly's chatter.

She popped the trunk lid of her ancient Cadillac, still in mint condition. The dome light illuminated a huge array of colorful garments in open shopping bags, the receipts resting on top.

Adam stood to one side, his brows curiously crunched together. Thankfully, he had the good manners not to ask the questions bouncing around in his head. I should have known from his earlier easy acceptance of my family, he wouldn't do anything to cause my aunt distress.

Impressed that the earlier razzing he had received from my brother and cousins hadn't fazed him in the least, my estimation of his character went up another notch.

"Personally, I thought you'd like this one best." Aunt Polly pulled out a purple flowered dress and held it under her chin before glancing in my direction. "And I got it at a very good price." She reached in and held out a navy dress with white trim. "But I'm kind of partial to this one too."

She turned to Adam. "What do you think, Adam? Which looks best? The purple or navy." She held up the purple garment under her chin, and then the navy one. "I know in this light you can't see how pretty it is, but you must take my word for it. Both are quite beautiful on."

He looked at me not knowing what to say then glanced back at Aunt Polly. "Is it for you?"

"Of course." She looked at him as if he was joking.

I turned my head so he wouldn't see the grin pulling at my lips.

Adam took his time examining both dresses. "I agree. The purple will look lovely on you."

"See, I told you this was the one." Her face beamed addressing me.

"Then I'd say it's sold."

I took the dress, folded, and put it back in the bag. "In fact, I'll take the other one too."

Adam's brows drew together in question as Aunt Polly rummaged around and then added shoes and purse to the bag.

She pulled out a sweater next.

"Mama picked this sweater out. I chose the pair of pants and the blouse knowing how much she liked them. There are also some unmentionables"—she glanced Adam's way—"which I won't pull out now. I figured you would want to buy them for her too."

"Certainly. The sweater and blouse are beautiful. And that pink will go well with Gram's white hair. Don't you agree, Adam?" I raised my brow, knowing Adam didn't have a clue as to what was going on.

"Yes, the pink would look nice."

I added another blouse, slacks, and a pair of shoes to my bag. After checking the receipts, I pulled money out of my pocket and handed the money to Aunt Polly to cover the cost of the presents.

"I'm afraid I don't have change." My aunt appeared worried.

"You keep it. It's a little something extra for your gas."

"Oh, I couldn't."

"Yes, you can. You saved me from having to go shopping."

She hugged me and planted a kiss on my cheek. "You're such a sweet girl."

Aunt Polly gave Adam a squint-eyed stare. "Young man, if you know what's what—and I'm sure you do—you won't let this one get away. Our Whitney is the best you'll ever find."

"Aunt Polly!" To say I was embarrassed was putting it mildly. The fire shot up my neck, flaming my cheeks. I felt like I had a fever. I averted my face.

"You're right. She is special." He put his arm around my waist and pulled me up next to him.

I wanted to push him away and would have, but his warmth felt too good. His nearness made me feel fuzzy, not realizing how I could be so affected just by a man's touch.

I didn't want to feel anything for Adam, knowing his feelings weren't involved. This wasn't an actual honest-to-goodness *you belong to me* thing. Yet, I couldn't fault his acting. He was superb.

"I knew you recognized our Whitney's worth." She leaned up on her tippy-toes, grabbing Adam by the shoulders, pulling him down to plant a kiss on his cheek, which he took graciously.

"You two make a lovely couple. Are you surprising Whitney with a ring for Christmas?"

"It wouldn't be a surprise if I told you, now would it?"

This guy was good, too good.

Aunt Polly laughed at Adam's pretend secret not knowing it was actually a save. How was she to know our relationship was anything but real? I knew if I told her otherwise, she wouldn't believe me.

"You two will make beautiful babies together."

"Aunt Polly, that's enough." I pulled away from Adam, grabbed the bags, and then shut the lid of her trunk.

Adam chuckled.

"Well, it's plain to me and everyone else. I'm just saying, dear."

"Adam and I are friends, nothing more."

"Hmm." She threw her little know-all look at me.

There was no way on earth that I would be able to dissuade her from her beliefs. Instead, I ended the conversation by rushing off toward Adam's car, my humiliation complete.

Aunt Polly continued chattering to Adam. Thankfully, I couldn't hear what she was saying. There's something to be said about *what you don't know can't hurt you,* or in my case, can't make you cringe.

67

Adam apparently pushed the remote to his car because it beeped when I arrived. Not knowing what to do with the packages since he didn't have a backseat, I slung the bags into the passenger area ready to shut the door.

I felt Adam long before I saw him. *Odd, how I was becoming so aware of the man.*

His hand wrapped over the top of the doorframe, his long, strong fingers effectively stopping me from slamming the door.

The sun had settled below the horizon making his face hard to read. Which meant he wouldn't be able to see my embarrassment either.

"Let's put those in the frunk"

"Frunk?"

"That's what Audi calls the front trunk."

"Makes sense … I guess." I was thankful he didn't bring up my Aunt's penchant for mistaken assumptions.

The frunk lid slowly opened. He took the packages from my hands and arranged the sacks to fit inside the small storage space.

"Sorry about my aunt."

"Don't be. She only has your interest at heart."

After closing the lid, he cocked his head to one side. "She wants to see you happy."

"I am happy."

"I know. But her idea of happiness for you is a husband and babies playing at your feet."

"She told you all of that?" I pounced my hands on my hips. Shaking my head, I released a breathy, "Oh, goodness."

"No, she didn't. But, if you remember, I have family also. Too many of them are like your Aunt Polly—wanting me to settle down with a wife and kids. They mean well, but like you, until that right person comes along, I choose to be single. But I don't mind playing along if it makes your aunt happy."

"Delusional is more like it."

Adam laughed. "There is that too."

Exhaling loudly, the weight lifted from my shoulders. "Thanks, Adam, for understanding. But I am *so* going to have a private talk with my aunt."

"You're welcome. But don't." Adam leaned against the car, his arms folded over his chest, his legs crossed at the ankles. "You know, she makes perfect sense."

"About what?"

"You." His attention solely on me, he turned serious. "You're attractive. You have a family who cares about you. You're intelligent. Your career is established. You handle yourself well, and love your family to distraction. And you're loyal. You would be the perfect woman for any man."

The warm and fuzzy began to creep back over me. "How do you figure that?"

He studied his shoes. "Which? That you're attractive and smart? Or that your family loves you and your brother would probably kill any man who would think of laying a hand on you." He chuckled. "I bet Seth wears a gun strapped to his ankle."

"That's a safe bet. He's a cop. His job has taught him to be overly cautious. And where I'm concerned, he's a bit overprotective." I smiled. "However, you don't know me well enough to know the rest."

"That's where you're wrong. Today has just confirmed what I knew to be true about you."

I let loose an unlady-like snort. "Not hardly."

"A man doesn't live next door to a very desirable woman and not learn a little about her, even if all we've said for the last two years is *hello*." He pushed off from the fender. "But you're shivering."

He opened the door of the car and motioned for me to climb in. "If we're going to continue this conversation, I'd rather do it out of sight of prying eyes and ears. Get in the car and I'll turn on the heater."

Knowing if we stayed out much longer, my brother would come looking for us, I shook my head.

"Better yet, why don't we go inside and tell everyone goodnight. We can talk on the way home."

He shrugged, shutting the door. "We can talk later. I don't want you to cut the evening short with your family."

"No, I'm ready to leave. It's been a long day." *Even on my nerves.*

He placed his hand at the small of my back. A tingling sensation zapped up my spine, which let me know that I wasn't as Adam-proof as I wanted to believe.

What woman in her right mind wouldn't feel some kind of spark with his touch?

When we walked inside, everyone stopped talking and smiled. I wondered what Aunt Polly had told them. No doubt filled their ears with a lot of nonsense about an engagement and babies.

"Sorry, y'all, but I have a ton of paperwork from my job back at my apartment that's calling my name."

Adam probably thought I lied with impunity. He stood there listening, not offering to add to my perceived sins.

I hadn't lied ... exactly. There were a lot of last minute details for the children's benefit that needed my attention. They just weren't urgent enough that I had to leave early. But, I did need to get them done, especially since I was losing Saturday by going with Adam.

I hugged all the relatives, telling them I'd see them at Christmas, if not sooner. I kissed Mom and Dad, received a bear hug from Seth, and a wet kiss from little Mandy.

Adam shook hands and talked as if they were all old friends, which made me feel good.

Seth, along with my parents, walked us to the door.

"Thanks for coming." Mom gave Adam a hug. "It's always a pleasure to have a friend of Whitney's join us for dinner. You come back soon now."

My dad clasped Adam's hand. "If you don't have plans for Christmas, we'd love to have you."

"Thank you. You're very kind."

"Can we expect to see Whitney wearing a ring soon?" Seth raised his brows staring down Adam.

A lesser man would have cowered. Not Adam.

He smiled. "A man doesn't disclose his business before all the negotiations are completed."

Whatever did that mean? Sounded like a lot of fancy footwork to me. The guy was good, I'd give him that.

I punch Seth. "Would you act your age?"

"I'm just watching out for you, is all." Again Seth gave Adam a long hard stare.

Most criminals under Seth's scrutiny would have been squirming by now. Not Adam.

"You don't have to worry of Whitney. She's safe with me."

Dad cleared his throat, causing Seth to back off.

"Goodnight. And thanks again for the lovely meal."

Mom beamed. "You're welcome. Glad you came."

As natural as breathing, Adam placed his hand at the small of my back and led me out of the house to the car.

Though I tried to think of it as a friendly, courteous gesture, my body didn't seem to understand.

How had I let this happen?

My emotions were tied into knots and yet, at the same time, bouncing all over the place.

Where Adam was concerned, I was one step away from tumbling head over heels off the proverbial cliff for the guy.

I had broken all the rules. My feelings were becoming way too involved with my neighbor.

Though it went against my grain to renege on a bargain, I would have to tell Adam all bets were off. I couldn't attend his family function, or for that matter any of the other functions. After all, he'd laid down the ground rules—no involvement. A rule my heart didn't seem to understand.

Chapter 9

"Do you have siblings?" We had just left my parents' house. Out of curiosity I wanted to learn more about the man.

Adam kept his eyes on the road, a quirky smile in place. "Just me until about fifteen years ago, then I inherited a step-sister who can be a real pain in the backside at times." He grinned.

"How so?"

"She's always sticking her nose into my business. But I've learned to ignore her. Lately, she's been trying to set me up with what she calls *suitable* women."

"Ah, I see. Must be the reason behind the Thanksgiving exchange." I gave him a sideway glance. "You think to throw her off the scent?"

"Something like that."

What would he say when I reneged on Saturday?

"Do you have cousins?" Anything to keep the conversation going. I glanced at the dark scenery zooming by outside the car.

"Out of the woodwork."

How could Adam's chuckle and his clean manly smell have my emotions zinging all over the place? Besides the obvious—considerate, handsome, fun to be with—I was attracted to him.

He wasn't my type. I never looked at guys other women would zero in on. Men like that were too self-absorbed. But Adam was different. He was personable and made me feel special, as if everything I had to say was important to him. Most guys would just zone out.

"You'll meet some of the Ryder, Clancy, and Morgan clan members on Saturday."

"Clancy and Morgan?"

"Clancy, my mother's side. Morgan, my stepmother's. My mother died when I was ten. For the last fifteen years on Thanksgiving weekend, whoever can make it from my mother's side will be there. And the same goes with my stepmother, Audrey's side. It's the one time of the year we see most of the family."

"Adam, about Saturday—"

"Hold that thought."

He pulled into the garage, parked the car, and then jogged around to open my door. I stood to the side while he opened the frunk and pulled out the bags filled with the Christmas gifts, which he wouldn't allow me to carry.

The closer we got to the elevators, my stomach clinched, and I wasn't sure if I could tell him.

"Once I drop these off, do you want to come to my apartment for our discussion?" He punched the floor number then waited for my answer.

"No, mine. I have hot chocolate, and right now I could use some."

"Yours it is then." His gaze held mine.

I wondered if he knew that I was going to back out of our bargain.

The elevator bell dinged, and the doors opened. We stepped into the hall and headed toward my apartment. The

74

only noise in the carpeted hallway was the swishing of bags.

I pulled out my card, swiped the reader, and opened the door.

"You can set those over there on the floor." I pointed to the door leading into my bedroom.

I filled the teakettle and prepared the cups, while Adam walked around the room looking at my artwork on the walls. I was too embarrassed to tell him I painted the pictures. Let him think what he would.

He turned and looked at me oddly. "Are these yours?"

"They're on my walls, aren't they?" I chuckled, hoping he hadn't guessed I'd painted them.

"You know what I mean. W. R. Singleton. Are you the artist?"

"Guilty as charged." I motioned to the overstuffed club chair. "Have a seat. The cocoa will be done as soon as the water boils."

"How long have you been painting?"

"Since high school. I keep my easel and paints in the spare bedroom. When I'm uptight or need something to occupy my mind or work out a weighty problem, I paint."

"You don't just paint. You're good enough to have your own studio."

I savored his compliment. "Thanks. But I'm hardly that good."

The high-pitched shrill of the teakettle blasted the room, giving me a reason to close an uncomfortable conversation. I was never easy with praise. And Adam's praise affected me differently than most. A real boost to my ego, as if I were truly an artist, one who could accomplish wonderful things with a stroke of a brush.

After preparing the two cups of hot chocolate, I topped them with marshmallows and inserted a spoon in each.

"Be careful, this is very hot, but good." I handed him the cup and a napkin and then went back for mine. When I

75

was finally settled in the other club chair facing him, I tried again, "About Saturday—"

"This hot chocolate is great. I've never tasted a powder mix this good."

"It's an old family recipe. In the fall, I make up a huge batch. That way, when I want a cup, it's as quick as boiling water."

"Now I know where to come for a hot cup of cocoa."

"Any time. Now about Saturday."

He tilted his head to the side, his gaze disconcerting. "Why do I get the idea you're trying to back out of our bargain and not go with me on Saturday."

"It's not that I don't want to go, I ..." I gnawed on my bottom lip, unable to come up with a plausible excuse. If I told him I was beginning to like him too much, that would go over like a stale cracker. Tasteless and unwanted.

"If you think I was offended by what your Aunt Polly said, I wasn't."

I stirred my cocoa. "I'm sorry about that. Talk about embarrassing. She knows better. And she's not batty, though at time she likes to play the eccentric."

"No worry. I like her." He laughed. "What's up with the packages in her trunk? I didn't want to ask for fear of offending her."

Taking a sip of my chocolate, I studied him over the rim of the cup before setting it down.

"Thanks for that." I released a breath. "It's a long story, but suffice it to say, when I was a little girl, Aunt Polly got tired of receiving gifts she didn't want or need. She always ended up taking them back to the store to exchange them. So, years ago she devised a plan. She buys what she and Grams want, then on Thanksgiving Day, everyone shops out of her trunk."

"No one thinks it's odd that she buys her own gifts? Not that I wouldn't love that sweet set up."

"Nope."

"Ingenious." He laughed. "I wished I'd thought of that. I hate to shop for others, especially when they give a person no hint of what they want."

"I know. It is rather nice not to have to wonder if they'll like it or not."

"Why not leave the gifts with her? Why bring them home?"

"To wrap them."

"Wrap them?" He looked baffled.

"Sure." I smiled thinking of Aunt Polly and her ritual. "Once they're wrapped, we bring them back to Mom's and Dad's and put them under the tree."

Adam shook his head as if this was the craziest thing he'd ever heard.

"We all have a good laugh when Grams opens her presents and is actually surprised. I don't think she remembers she picked out her own gifts."

"And Aunt Polly?"

"*Well*, Aunt Polly is Aunt Polly. She goes through this elaborate ruse of trying to guess what's in each package. She shakes it, sniffs it, even squeezes it. We're all in stiches by the time she finally opens the present.

"One year for fun, I wrapped up a pair of men's boxer shorts just to see what she'd do. At first, she looked shocked. Then she got even with me by wearing the boxers over her slacks and threatened to go out in public with them on. It was priceless, but taught me a lesson." Feeling a little embarrassed, I added, "To get the full affect, you would've had to been there to see her performance."

"I'd love to. When does this all take place? Christmas morning or Christmas Eve?"

Unsure if he thought I had just invited him and he'd accepted, I figured the best way to proceed was to ignore his assumption and answer his question.

"We open gifts Christmas Eve." I cradled the now warm chocolate in the palms of my hands. "A tradition we

77

started when I was eight. Since I was the youngest, I didn't want to wait. Seth and Shelly were beyond Santa Clause. So they talked me into declaring I didn't want to wait to open my presents. I wanted them now."

I shook my head, the memory fresh in my mind. "You should have seen my parent's face. Especially after I told them I had found all the presents under their bed and knew there wasn't a real Santa Claus anyway."

"What did your folks do?"

"They threatened I'd get nothing for Christmas except a lump of coal if I didn't go to bed. Needless to say, I went to bed." I smiled over the fond memory.

"You must have been a handful."

"Still am."

"So you got your way?"

"Two years later." I wrinkled my nose. "But no better than I deserved after giving them an ultimatum."

"." His sparkling eyes told me he felt no pity.

"If you're not careful, you'll get a lump of coal in your stocking."

"Ah, but you don't believe in Santa Claus."

"That's true, but it doesn't mean that you won't get a lump of coal. I have connections. I know a person, who knows a person, who knows—"

"—who knows a person. I get it." He laughed.

"Now you're catching on. So you better be nice."

I really enjoyed Adam's company.

"What about Saturday? Please don't back out on me now, not after I sat through a full day of interrogation. Your brother and cousins were merciless, not to mention the few times your father and uncles chimed in. Any moment I felt they would place me on the rack." His dazzling eyes were filled with merriment.

"They weren't that bad. I heard a lot of laughing from the living room while I was in the kitchen slaving away."

"They water boarded me into submission. Your brother threatened to haul me off to jail if I didn't cooperate. I had to tell them everything they wanted to know."

I rolled my eyes. "Feed me another one."

"If you don't believe me, ask them."

"Adam, I don't think—"

"I'm not asking you to think, just don't back out on me now."

I knew I was asking for trouble. Yet, I couldn't refuse.

He stood, drained the last bit of cocoa, and then licked a tiny bit of marshmallow from his lips. "I'd better leave so you can get your work done. Thanks for the cocoa. That stuff is addictive. I may be pounding on your door for more."

"Anytime. Glad you like it." I followed him, wondering about his abrupt goodbye.

"Thanks for not standing me up. I'll pick you up at noon on Saturday." Grinning, he leaned toward me, kissed me on the cheek, and was out the door.

My hand automatically went to my face, covering the imprint of his soft lips.

It wasn't a lover's kiss. More like a really close friend showing their appreciation. But my heart didn't care. I was falling for this guy in the worst way.

Chapter 10

How can I be so assertive at my job and in other areas in my life, yet, so cowardly pathetic when it comes to Adam Ryder? I didn't want to go with him to his parents' house, but I didn't have the nerve to refuse him. The only reasonable explanation ... he had twisted the screws and ...

No, that was a bald-faced lie. There was no way I would stand him up after he'd so graciously taken so much grief from my family.

That wasn't completely the truth either. Though I knew there wasn't a future with Adam, I wanted to be with him even if it were only friendship.

I stood in my bedroom amidst utter chaos. In less than an hour, Adam would be knocking on my door expecting me to look presentable and not like a pathetic lunatic just released from bedlam.

My breakfast threatened to come up every time I thought about meeting his family. I didn't know what to expect. Maybe they would think I wasn't good enough for him. However, it didn't matter since we were nothing more than quasi friends and a plus-one through the holidays.

The fit I was about to throw could be chalked up to having dinner with perfect strangers. I knew his family would speculate whether or not we were an item, just like mine had.

I rummaged around on the bed to find the black and white maxi-skirt and black sweater—the very first item I'd tried on. Both could be perceived as dressy or casual enough, which should fit the occasion. I slipped on several long strands of pearls, a pearl and silver bracelet, and finished with large pearl eardrops.

Thankfully, I had finished my hair and makeup before dressing. Otherwise, I would have been late, which smacked of self-importance.

I freshened my hair and my lipstick, and was changing my purse when the doorbell rang.

A quick look at the clock meant Adam was five minutes early. Thankfully, I was ready. I marched to the front and proceeded to open the door.

My smile faltered and turned to ash.

"Hey, Whit." Jeremy leaned in pulling me toward him and planted a kiss on my cheek.

It would have been on my lips if I hadn't turned my face at the last second. "What are you doing here?"

"I was in the neighborhood and thought I'd stop by and see if you'd like to go for some coffee? I have something important to discuss with you."

"I'm afraid she can't. Her day is already filled." The gruff sound of Adam's voice and the menacing look in his beautiful eyes made my heart skip a beat. Thankfully, his gaze was directed at Jeremy.

"Who are you?" Jeremy glared at Adam.

"I would ask the same of you, but I already know." Adam bared his teeth in a snarl of a smile. "You're Whitney's ex, emphasis on ex."

"Why you—"

"Are you ready, hon?" When Adam looked at me, his expression was filled with love, which nearly floored me. His endearment left me too stunned to answer until I saw the prompting in his gaze.

"Ah-yes. Yes, I am." I turned to Jeremy. "As you can see, I'm on my way out. And furthermore, we said all there was to say six months ago. There's nothing more to be said. Have a good life if you can."

"Whitney?" Jeremy looked as if he'd swallowed a fish whole with the scales going down the wrong way.

Stepping over the threshold caused Jeremy to step back. Adam moved smoothly between him and me and pulled the door shut.

"Shall we?" He motioned for me to precede him, effectively keeping Jeremy behind us.

We moved toward the elevator, Adam's hand at my back. I felt the tension in him. Thankfully, not directed at me. This was one time I wished I lived on the ground floor for a quick getaway.

Adam pushed the button, which produced an immediate ding as the elevator doors opened. We stepped on board. He pushed the ground floor button, and the doors began to close.

We were home free. No more confrontation with Jeremy.

A hand flashed in between the doors, causing them to jerk to a stop and then open again.

On walked Jeremy, a cocksure smile in place.

An uneasy silence filled the little cube as the soft hum of the elevator motor began our descent.

"And just how long have you known Whitney?" Jeremy smacked of overconfidence.

"Going on two years now." Adam smiled down at me. His arm around my waist tightened and pulled me up close and away from my ex.

"She never mentioned you to me."

"And why would she?" Adam raised a threatening brow. "She did mention you in passing, but not in glowing terms."

"Why you …" Jeremy advanced on Adam.

Adam pushed me in the corner behind him, his body shielding me.

"I wouldn't do that if I were you."

Hearing Adam's voice was a revelation. I'd never heard him use such a menacing tone before. And though I couldn't see his face, I imagined it was as fierce as his voice, and no doubt, the reason why Jeremy backed down.

Thankfully the elevator stopped. Yet, the doors didn't open fast enough.

Even though he was willing, I didn't want Adam forced to defend me. We were barely friends after all.

I peeked around Adam's broad shoulder and was about to step out from behind him when his hand stopped me. I stayed put.

"You first." He motioned for Jeremy to exit.

Jeremy spoke a couple of choice words, words I'd never heard him utter while in my presence, then he walked out—hopefully out of my life for good.

Adam stepped aside, held out his hand to stop the closing doors. "You ready?"

"Sure."

Up until this moment I hadn't realized just how much Jeremy's threatening presence had frayed my nerves. My legs were wobbly. I wasn't sure I could walk off the elevator without Adam's help.

He must have noticed, because he took my hand, gave a tender squeeze, and then slid his arm around my waist to lead me out into the hall.

From out of nowhere, a fist connected with Adam's upper cheek.

He shoved me out of harms' way as he flew backwards against the wall, but still standing. He recovered faster than I thought possible.

Seeing I stood between him and Jeremy, Adam grabbed my arm and pushed me away, ready to take another blow.

It didn't happen.

Adam, like a prized wrestler, latched onto Jeremy's fist, clamping down on it like a vice. And then he pulled it around and up behind Jeremy's back, nearly twisting his arm off, while the little coward whined and writhed with pain.

"You can either leave here peaceably, or …" He pulled up on Jeremy's arm causing him to squeal louder. "I can continue to hold you while Whitney calls the police to come haul your sorry backside off to jail." Adam's words were grounded out through clinched teeth.

"Let go of me. You're breaking my arm." Jeremy sounded pleading and in pain.

Adam pulled Jeremy's arm up even higher causing the guy to clamp down hard on his jaw, effectively cutting off a yell.

"All right. All right. I'll leave. Just let me go."

"Good." Adam didn't release him. "But first we'll have an understanding."

"Anything, man. Let up. You're breaking my arm."

Adam rolled his eyes. "You are never to come here again. And you will not contact Whitney either by phone, text, or in person." He yanked Jeremy's arm again. "Do you understand me?"

"Yes, man. Let me go."

"Good." Continuing to hold on to Jeremy, Adam glanced back at me. "You stay here. And if I don't come back, call 911."

Too stunned to say anything, I nodded and began searching in my purse for my cell phone. My hand shook, making it difficult to find the illusive phone, while keeping a watch on Adam.

He quickstepped Jeremy to the front and then shoved him out the door.

Jeremy stumbled a few feet, before becoming stable, and then turned to look at Adam.

I moved in their direction afraid Jeremy would start up again.

He didn't. But if Jeremy's venomous look could have killed, Adam's folks would have been planning his funeral. And this was all my fault.

Without a word, Adam came back inside, yanked on the cuffs of his leather jacket, and then smiled before ushering me toward the front doors.

"My car's out front. I brought it around earlier thinking this would be easier. I wasn't expecting company." He gave a half grin, then winced, his hand touching the huge red spot where Jeremy had sucker punched him.

"Here, let me see." I reached up and gently touched his chin, turning his profile to me. The shock of his soft warm skin with a hint of whiskers felt good beneath my fingers. His cologne tickled my nose and sent my senses zinging off the chart. My hand fell away.

"He didn't tear the skin, thankfully." I was surprised I could even talk.

Adam grunted. "Not for want of trying."

"I'm so sorry. This is all my fault."

His heated gaze stopped me from saying more.

"Don't you even think about taking the blame. It was all Jeremy's doing. Only a coward would punch a guy when he's not looking."

"I agree. But you need to put some ice on your cheek to take down the swelling. I've got an ice pack in my freezer. I'll go up and get it."

I turned to leave but his hand on my arm stopped me.

"It's fine. If it gets to feeling worse, I'll get some ice at Dad's."

My shame knew no bounds. I would have to face his family while he explained to them how my ex-boyfriend nearly punched out his lights. Hesitating, I said, "Adam, I can't go and face your family. I'm too humiliated. I—"

He put a finger to my lips. "I understand. But my folks are expecting you." A sweet, innocent frown appeared. "You can't leave me in a lurch to face them alone. What will that do to my reputation?"

I rolled my eyes. "Nothing."

"That's what you think. They'll have a great laugh at my expense and poke fun at me for my date being a no-show. Come on. Help a guy out here. Please."

Unable to meet his clear blue eyes, I lowered my gaze.

He lifted my chin, staring at me square in the face.

I began to squirm.

"I want you to get it through your head … none of this was your fault. You just happened to have the misfortune to have dated a jerk, and by default I met him." He rubbed his cheek. "I'm glad I was here. No telling what that guy would have done otherwise."

"What will you tell your family?" I wanted to look away but his gaze held mine.

"That I met a guy who didn't like my looks and wanted to rearrange my face. More, they don't need to know."

Chapter 11

To say the drive was uncomfortable, put it mildly. Again, I tried to apologize for Jeremy's behavior. Adam wouldn't allow it. Yet, I felt I was solely responsible for Jeremy's little show of testosterone and Adam's bruised cheek.

We turned on the street to his family's house. That's when I realized they lived in the Swiss Avenue historic district of Dallas. Huge old mansions and homes from the turn of the century lined the road. I figured Adam's family came from wealthy ancestors or were rich enough to buy into the neighborhood. Either way, they were out of my league.

He slowed and then turned into a drive full of cars before he stopped the Audi, straddling the sidewalk of one of the largest, extraordinary houses we had passed on the street. The home was a stunning two-story, reddish-brown bricked Georgian style mansion with white trim, cornices, and shutters. A wide walkway, consisting of several landings with steps leading up to the entrance, stopped at a covered porch with impressive oversized, leaded-glass double doors leading into the house.

By the number of cars, this appeared to be more than just your—what was it Adam called it? Holiday/starter-bash/Thanksgiving? I tried to swallow my panic.

Bolstering my confidence with an inner pep talk wasn't going well. A boatload of concerns had been dumped in my stomach. *Why had I agreed to do this in the first place?*

"You can get out here. I'll park the car. That way you won't have to walk as far."

The house on its own was more than intimidating, not to speak of the hoards of people waiting inside. I shook my head. "No, I'd rather walk with you, if it's all the same."

"They won't bite." He grinned.

"I know, but …" How could I tell him I'd rather face a room of ugly donors than to face his family and friends alone.

"All right. Stick with me." After backing out, he moved on down the line of parked cars and found a place a couple of houses away.

As we walked back toward the house, I glanced up. The sight was breathtaking. I couldn't imagine living in such a place.

"Have your folks lived here long?"

"Afraid so. My great-grandfather built the house back in the early 1920s. And a Ryder has lived here since."

"That's incredible. I can't imagine what it would be like to live with that much history and be responsible for its upkeep."

"The maintenance comes with a hefty price tag. These old beauties are a constant outlay of cash."

"Gorgeous doesn't adequately describe your parent's house." I flourished my hand about. The whole place smacked of wealth.

Though most plants were dormant for the winter, purple and red pansies wove a pretty pattern along the walkway. Poinsettias lined both sides of the wide expanse of steps and landings leading up to the front entrance. Huge wreaths hung on the front doors and the windows across the front.

I glanced over at Adam, and had to ask the question that had been festering in my mind since the night on the balcony. "Why did you make the bargain?"

"The one-plus thing?" He cocked his brow.

"Yes. You're a good-looking man—"

"Thank you, I think." His gorgeous dimples appeared.

"That was meant as a compliment. And the question remains, why did you offer?"

"Truthfully?"

"Yes, please."

"I wanted to get to know you better."

"You could have come over to my place anytime and said *hi, can we be friends.* So why now?"

He tugged on my arm to stop me. We were halfway up the front steps on the middle landing.

"You're sure full of questions."

I tilted my head, studying him without saying anything, trying my best to understand the motive behind the man.

He shrugged. "For the last two years we've passed in the halls saying hello. I liked what I saw. The other night was the perfect opportunity to get to know you better." He didn't make a move to climb the remaining steps.

"Like I said, you could have—"

"Ah, but would you have gone out with me?"

Stunned that he'd figured me right, I didn't know what to say.

"I thought not." There was no rancor in his voice, just a matter of fact. "I've watched you for the past two years and know a lot about you."

"Like what?"

"For instance, you're not a party girl."

"A party girl?" I wrinkled my nose exhibiting my distaste. "Hardly."

"That makes you unlike most women I know."

"Should I be flattered?"

"Probably. Yes." He nodded. "You were always polite when we met. And just like the other night, when you were afraid I would hurt you're aunt's feelings, you were ready to step in, just in case. That says a lot about your character. And it told me something else."

"What was that?"

"You're someone I would like to know better and see where it goes."

He slid my hand in his as if it was the natural thing to do, then waited to see if I would resist. Satisfied when I didn't, we started climbing the front steps again.

Our hands together felt normal. Yet, I was afraid he'd feel the tremble of excitement in mine. I worked hard to act normal while telling my nerves to simmer down.

His words had flattered and thrilled, but also worried me. I didn't know Adam. *Yeah*, sure I'd seen him casually for the last two years … nothing more. Did I want more out of this friendship, if that's what this was? Did I want to date him?

More to the question … was he serious? Or was I just a distraction for him. And then there was the huge matter of Lori. Was she just a friend?

"Wow, for once you're speechless."

"I'm a little taken back." Seeing we had reached the front door, I added, "And we don't have time to discuss this now."

"Later then, when we have more time." He raised his brows. "Like tonight when I take you home."

I nodded, more confused than ever.

Adam opened the door to the house and stood back as I entered.

The entry held a 15-foot fully decked Christmas tree. Lighted garland hung from the staircase handrails, while the aroma of mulled spices filled the air. If I hadn't thought of Christmas before today, I certainly was now. Everything in the house spoke of the Christmas season from the beautiful ornate nativity on the table at the side of the huge tree to the music being lightly piped into the room.

Voices came from a room to our right and also somewhere from the back of the house.

He placed his hand to the small of my back. Though it felt right, I wasn't sure I would ever get used to his touch.

Leading me to the right, I figured I was about to meet his family.

Why I was nervous, I had no idea. This meant nothing to him, or for that matter to me … much.

The living room, filled with several groupings of comfortable looking chairs and loveseats were all occupied. Others were standing, talking. There were a whole lot more people than what Adam was subjected to at my family gathering.

As with my folks, the whole room fell silent, and everyone turned to stare as we entered.

One man with graying temples, wearing glasses, looked to be an older version of Adam. He pulled away from a group of men and headed in our direction with his deep dimples showing. At the same time, a graceful, very attractive woman, brown hair hanging around her shoulders, bangs blunt-cut, rose from her chair.

"Son." His father clapped him on the back, pulling him into a bear hug.

"Adam, you made it." The woman slipped her hand on his shoulder, tipped up, and kissed his cheek. She touched the small knot that had formed on his jaw. Though she didn't ask, her gaze questioned.

"It doesn't hurt. Just a clumsy accident."

"We were beginning to worry about you." His father said good-naturedly while staring at me.

"Dad, Audrey, I'd like you to meet Whitney Singleton." He turned. "Whitney, this is my father and stepmother, Jim and Audrey Ryder."

"Whitney, we're happy to meet you and so glad that you could come to our little gathering." Audrey gave me a hug and then glanced at Adam. "Where have you been keeping this lovely woman?" She didn't wait for an answer, just turned and dragged me further into the living room.

"Everyone, I would like you to meet Adam's friend, Whitney Singleton." She turned to me. "We'll dispense with names for now. There are way too many to remember, but you will eventually meet everyone before you leave. However, I want you to meet Adam's grandfather. He's been a widower for three years now. He'll be anxious to meet you."

I looked back for Adam as I was being dragged across the room, but he and his father were in deep discussion.

Just look at this as one of your charity functions. I plastered a smile on my face ready to do the pleasantries.

If anyone would have asked me to guess which one was Grandfather Ryder, I could have easily picked him out of the crowd. When we approached, a white haired man rose from a wingback chair. His blue eyes, though faded, sparkled much like Adam's. The Ryder dimples—by now I could plainly see where they came from—were even more pronounced than his son's or grandson's.

"Grandpa Ryder, this is Whitney Singleton, Adam's friend."

I didn't miss the raised brow Audrey gave Adam's grandfather nor her huge smile.

Gathering my hand in his, he patted the top of mine. "Nice to meet you, Whitney. Where has Adam been hiding you?" He released me, looking past my shoulder.

What exactly was I supposed to say to that? "I wasn't exactly hiding." I smiled.

"That grandson of mine should have brought you around long before now. I hope I can soon say—"

"Grandpa." Adam grabbed the older man up into a bear hug, whispered something in his ear, and then released the man, stepping back. "I see you've met Whitney. If you don't mind, I'm going to borrow her for a few minutes to introduce her to the cousins."

I would never know what Grandpa Ryder was about to say. Adam latched onto my hand, led me out into the vestibule, and down a hall, into a large solarium. The room was full of young adults about our age, with a sprinkling of children and a few teens over in the corner talking.

"Hey, everyone."

The noise stopped and all eyes were on us again.

"I want you to meet Whitney." He turned and winked at me.

Stunned, but figuring his wink meant nothing more than teasing, I smiled.

Since the moment I walked into the house, I seemed to be the object of interest and speculation. It shouldn't have bothered me. Adam had gone through much the same with my family—stares, smiles, knowing nods, and raised brows—except at my function Adam had received a full-fledged interrogation, which thankfully I hadn't, and hopefully wouldn't.

While talking with one of Adam's cousins, the room fell silent, much like when I had walked in with Adam, only this time, the room zinged with electricity, as if something was about to take place.

When I turned to see what had caused the stir of expectancy, I felt Adam stiffen next to me.

A gorgeous, leggy blonde, her dress hugging her body, looked a lot like one of my beloved Barbie dolls of old. She hung on the arm of a man about Adam's size and age. His slicked-back light brown hair and scruffy beard reminded me of Justin Timberlake's, but his smile reminded me of Adam's, just not as handsome.

I glanced up in time to witness the distaste in Adam's eyes, which told me he wasn't happy that this couple had shown up, but I didn't know why.

They headed straight for us. I wasn't sure if I should excuse myself or stay anchored to his side. Yet, I felt Adam's tension build the nearer they got.

Without another thought, I ran my arm through Adam's, and moved as close to him as decency would allow. Why? I had no clue. I just knew he needed me, and I wanted to let Adam know I was there for him.

When he didn't shrug me off, I figured we were good.

Instead, he placed his hand over mine reassuringly. That's when it dawned on me like a full harvest moon in autumn. This wasn't going to be a pleasant encounter. This man and woman meant something to Adam, or at least they had at one time, and still did, even if he might not want to admit it.

"Adam." The Justin look-alike tentatively stuck out his hand. "I wasn't sure you'd be here."

"Hello, Michael. And why wouldn't I be here? Though I don't live here, this is my parents' home."

Michael's laugh sounded strained and tinny. "You're right, of course."

After accepting Michael's handshake, Adam nodded at the woman. "Brittney." His expression was without emotion. "I would have thought you wouldn't be here, though. Weren't you on a honeymoon?" His words were directed to Michael.

Michael looked uncomfortable while Adam appeared indifferent. However, the trace of irritation coming from him, along with the tension I felt in his arm said differently.

"Well ... I—" Michael shifted nervously while Brittney gave me the once over and then sniffed like she smelled something bad in the air before glancing away bored.

I thought maybe this might be a good time for me to leave and give the three of them some privacy. However, Adam had a different idea.

He kept a firm grip on my hand that was still latched through his arm. While giving me a knock-you-off-your-feet smile, I saw the hurt in his gaze.

"Whitney, hon, I would like you to meet my cousin Michael and his bride Brittney. While growing up, Michael and I were inseparable. We shared everything … our toys, our cars, we even shared … well let's suffice it to say, we were close." Adam looked adoringly at me as if we were truly in love.

It wasn't hard to smile back or to pretend we were, which seemed to have worked if the daggers Brittney was throwing my way meant anything. I had a sinking feeling this woman had belonged to Adam at one time. Or maybe I was misreading everyone's vibes, but I didn't think so.

Holding out my hand, first to Michael, I said, "So nice to finally meet you."

The couple's surprise wasn't lost on me.

I was happy to help him out of this awkward situation, if this was truly an old girlfriend his cousin stole away. I'd been on the receiving end of rejection and knew how it felt.

"How long have you two been dating?" Brittney couldn't keep the hate from her voice.

"A while now." Adam turned to smile down at me.

"Whitney!" Lori walked around the couple, leaned in and gave me a hug. "I didn't know you had arrived. I've been working in the kitchen."

What was Lori doing here?

Duh! Lori Morgan, Adam's stepsister.

Relief surged through me. I was a ninny for not realizing it sooner. "We arrived a little bit ago."

"I was wondering when you and my big brother would get here." Lori turned to Adam and gave him a hug and a kiss on the cheek.

A knowing look passed between Adam and Lori, one of unity.

95

She turned to face Michael and Brittney, hooking her arm in mine. I was effectively sandwiched between her and Adam.

"Well, I see the happy couple is back from the honeymoon." Lori beamed over at Michael and Brittney. "Cut it short, huh?" She raised her brows, a smirk riding her lips.

"Brittney wanted to be home in time for the Thanksgiving bash. So we flew in yesterday."

"How nice. Welcome back." Lori turned to Adam. "If you don't mind, I sure could use your help in the other room."

Uncertain if I was to stay behind or go with them, Lori pulled me forward. I barely got out *nice to meet you* before I was whisked out of the room and down the hall into the kitchen.

Lori let go of my arm and turned to Adam. "I'm sorry. I wasn't able to let you know they were coming. I just found out from mom a few minutes ago."

"Doesn't matter. I'm not invested in either of them. They made their bed and they can have it." He sounded tired of the subject.

Adam gazed down at me. "I'm sorry you were shoved into the middle of all that. But thanks for staying by my side."

"Glad I could help."

No doubt, seeing the questions in my eyes, he took my hand. "As much as I hate to admit it, Brittney and I once dated. What I saw in her, I'll never know."

"Up until you wouldn't give her what she wanted—a ring on her finger, your name, and a no limit credit line." Lori made a scoffing sound of disgust.

"Lori." He scowled at his sister.

"It's true. It's a shame Michael wasn't as smart as you."

"That's enough." His stern voice curtailed Lori's flow of words.

"A lot of what Lori said is true. However, you can rest assured, Brittney holds no appeal, and hasn't for a long time now, if she ever truly did."

"Oh, I'm so excited that Adam and you are dating."

Lori's bubbly voice made me cringe. "We're—"

"We're taking it a day at a time, little one."

"Well I don't care. I told you Sunday, Whitney would be perfect for you." She grabbed my hand, held it out. "And now here you are." She released my fingers to give me another big hug. "Now, you two can help me serve these finger foods to the grownups."

"And what do you think we are? Turnips?" He wrinkled his nose.

Laughing, I said, "I'll help. What can I do?"

I was eager to do anything to get away from the awkward situation. No matter that it meant serving food to strangers who would be staring at me, thinking I belonged to Adam when I knew good and well, I didn't.

Chapter 12

The rest of the day, into the early evening, almost went without a hitch. I encountered Brittney once after our initial meeting. Coming out of the powder room, I practically ran the woman down.

She stood with her legs apart, her arms crossed, glaring at me. Instead of moving aside to let me pass, she blocked my way, sneering. At least, that's what her screwed up face and narrowed-eyed stare looked like.

"I don't know what little game you're playing, but I can tell you right now, Adam doesn't love you. He's not the marrying kind." She paused.

Without a comeback, I raised my brows as if I didn't know what she was talking about.

"Adam is cold-hearted and incapable of loving anyone or anything except himself and his job."

Refusing to lower myself to her level of cattiness, I smiled sweetly doing my best not to let her get under my skin.

"In fact, you're not his type." Her smile was cold, calculating.

That did it! Adam may hate me tomorrow, but … "I'm sorry you feel that way. However,"—I paused for effect—"Adam has always been a very warm and loving man to me. He's never once put his job first. Apparently, he's changed since you dated him." I wanted to snatch my words back.

"What has he told you?" Her brows drew together as she bit her lower lip.

Whoa! Was I ever off the hook on that one.

"Honestly, I can say Adam has never discussed you with me. A woman just knows these things. If you'll excuse me please." Feeling good about defending Adam, I stepped around her. Then as an afterthought, I threw over my shoulder. "Oh, by the way, congratulations, on your nuptials. I wish Michael and you happiness and the very best."

I meant the words too. I couldn't think of anything more miserable than to be stuck in an unhappy marriage.

All the way down the hall, I could feel her eyes boring holes in my back, singeing my insides. Though I walked sedately, I wanted to run. I couldn't reach the living room fast enough.

Note to self: Ask Adam why Creuella hates his guts—now you're being catty and unkind.

After my little one-on-one visit with Brittney, Adam must have sensed something was wrong. Maybe he saw Brittney follow me out of the hall. I don't know. But for whatever reason, he stayed by my side most of the day.

Whenever he left for any reason, Lori or her mother would magically appear, taking his place. To say they gave me the royal treatment, was putting it mildly.

Grandpa Ryder came over and sat down beside me on the loveseat.

"I've told Adam, he needed to find a good woman and settle down. It looks like he's finally taken my advice." He patted my hand. "Have you two set a date yet?"

"A date?"

He raised his brows and nodded, tapping his nose.

I scrambled for an answer when I saw the teasing glint in his eyes.

"I believe you know good and well we haven't set a date. We're just friends."

"Well, all I have to say … my grandson better step up his game, or he'll shame the Ryder name."

"How so?"

"Well, the first time my father laid eyes on my mother, he fell in love. They were married ten days later. When I saw my Bessie …" He swallowed, staring at his hands.

I laid my hand on the back of his.

"You're a sweet girl." He patted me.

Chuckling lightly, I said, "Hardly a girl. But thank you."

He waived me off. "Semantics." He breathed in. "As I was saying, when I saw Bessie, I knew right off she was the only one for me … and still is."

His sweet smile tugged at my heart as he looked off at some unseen memory.

"Now Bessie, she was a no nonsense gal. When I popped the question, she thought I was nuts. We'd only known each other a couple of days." He shook his head, chuckling, his eyes sparkling. "We eloped two weeks later. It lasted until she …" He glanced off.

"Even Jim there"—He pointed to Adam's father—"He asked Adam's mom on their second date." He winked at me and pointed at the entryway. "Yup. The moment you walked in that door with Adam, I knew."

Stunned to silence, I knew where he was headed, but I didn't know how to stop him. I didn't want to hurt his feelings for making the wrong assumption.

He nodded toward Adam. "There's just something about the way Adam looks at you. If he hasn't already asked, he will."

I kept silent. No use in spoiling his day. He'd find out soon enough he was wrong.

"What are you two talking about?" Adam looked so handsome in his blue sweater and khaki pants, it was hard not to drool.

Grandpa Ryder gave my hand a squeeze then stood and motioned for Adam to take his place. "Nothing much. Just telling Whitney here about the Ryder tradition." He glanced around. "I need to speak with your dad. Keep Whitney company while I'm gone." His eyes sparkled. "Thanks for listening to an old man ramble. Not many young women would have."

"Anytime. I enjoyed our talk."

He gave me a wink before walking off.

Adam didn't sit down, instead he held out his hand toward me. "I believe I'm ready to leave. How about you."

I shrugged. "I'm ready when you are."

"Good, I'll make our excuses and take you home."

Lori rushed up and took a hold of my hand. "It looks like my brother wants to whisk you off. I didn't want to miss saying goodbye." She hugged me. "I'm so glad you came."

"Hey, don't I warrant a hug?" Adam tapped Lori on the shoulder.

"Certainly." She gave him a squeeze then turned back to me. "If this big lug doesn't chase you off, I hope you will come again."

"Hey, watch who you're calling a *big lug.*"

"Whatever." Lori rolled her eyes dismissing her brother. "In fact, I'll give you a call one day next week and maybe we can go to lunch or dinner."

"Sure. That gives me an idea. I've been left in charge of the children's Christmas pageant at church. I could sure use some extra hands. Would you want to help?"

"Sounds like fun. Sure."

"I've enlisted my sister and brother to help me on Thursday night to get the props and costumes organized. If you could help that night too, it would be great. The more the merrier."

"Count me in." Lori appeared glad I had asked.

"You didn't ask me." Adam tried to look offended but missed the mark.

I figured he was teasing and not really interested. "I—"

"In fact, tell everyone not to eat dinner. I'll bring salad and pizza and we can eat before we start, say six-thirty. How does that sound?"

"You don't have to do that."

"Oh, yes he does. Getting to spend time with my big brother, him buying pizza, and seeing him do actual labor for once, should be interesting." She chuckled.

"I'll make you think work." He pulled her into a tight squeeze, then released her, smiling.

"I'm so glad you two are ..." She waved her hand at the both of us. "Well, you know."

I didn't know.

"Later, little sister." He took my arm and steered me toward his parents.

After saying our goodbyes to everyone, we stepped out on the porch. He had just closed the door when it opened again.

"Adam." It was Michael. "Could we meet sometime next week?"

"Next week?"

Michael glanced back at the door and then at Adam again. "Yes. I would like ... well, I'd like to talk with you ... just the two of us."

"Give me a call on Monday. We'll set something up."

"Thanks. I'll do that."

Looking relieved, Michael turned to me. "It was really nice meeting you, Whitney."

"Thank you."

"Goodnight." Michael entered the house and shut the door.

We walked down the steps and all the way to the car in silence. I would be lying if I said I wasn't a little curious, because I was. Yet, I didn't want to butt in. I knew Adam and Brittney had been an item, but how serious, I didn't know.

He helped me into the car, walked around and got in but didn't start the engine. "I'm sorry you had to be dragged into that drama."

"Don't worry. I can take drama as long as it comes in small spurts." I grinned.

"Do you mind if my explanation waits until we get home?"

"Sure, if you don't mind if I lean back, close my eyes, and relax."

"You deserve to rest after what you went through."

"Thanks. But it wasn't all that bad. Mine was easy compared to you with my brother and cousins. They were a whole lot worse."

His deep chuckle went all through me, melting any resistance to his charm. He was becoming much more than a friend. However, I didn't want to think about where our relationship was headed, at least not yet. I hardly knew the guy.

I closed my eyes. My body wouldn't settle down, not with this hunk sitting so close to me. And then there was the little question of Brittney.

Chapter 13

The streetlights flickered across my eyelids as Adam zoomed down the freeway toward our apartments.

"I enjoyed my visit with your family. And your grandfather ..." I chuckled. "He's a sweet man."

"He sure fell in love with you." Adam turned the car into our underground parking. "Did he also tell you how I was letting the Ryder men down?"

"He mentioned something about that."

"Hmm, I bet he did. And did he tell you how I haven't met a woman yet that I wanted to ask to marry me within days or weeks of meeting her?"

"I don't think that was mentioned." I was glad he couldn't see my face.

"I figured as much, because that news would've had you running out the door."

The heat rose even more to my cheeks remembering Grandpa Ryder words ... *the way Adam looks at you, if he hasn't already asked, he will.* The only thing I could think to say, "I'm made of sterner stuff."

"That's what I like about you." He parked, turned off the motor, and then stared at me.

I sat up, smoothing down my hair in back before grabbing my purse.

"You're different ... special."

"Nothing special here." Feeling uncomfortable beneath his stare, I said, "Shall we go in?"

"Sure."

He hopped out and came around to open my door. Again with his hand on my spine we walked to the elevators. This time, his touch felt intimate, close, even loving. Maybe I was too tired and reading more into the moment than was actually there. Or maybe it was because we were heading back to our apartments.

Whatever, I didn't want to feel close with Adam. Nor did I want my feelings all tied up in a knot, being unsure.

We were silent in the elevator and even as he walked me to my door.

"Do you think I could have another cup of your hot chocolate?"

I wanted to say no—to get away from him and the romantic ideas forming in my head.

"Sure. I'd like one too. Come on in." I opened the door, stepped out of my shoes and shoved them under the hall table. I made my way to the kitchen to turn the fire on under the teakettle.

Adam, hands in pant pockets, walked over to the fireplace. He stood studying my painting over the mantle.

"I really love this piece. I need something like it over my fireplace." He turned to stare at me. "Could I commission you to paint one for me?"

"Oh, no. I don't do that." Shaking my head, hoping he wouldn't insist, I said, "I've never painted for hire, just pleasure. Not sure that I could. Being paid to paint would take away the enjoyment."

"Think about it. I'd be willing to pay a hefty fee if you did."

The shrilly whistle of the teakettle interrupted the conversation. I hoped he would forget about asking me.

While I made the cocoa, Adam moved to the patio door, opened it, and stood looking out over the city.

I came up behind him and handed him his cup of cocoa. "Do you feel like sitting outside?"

"Sure." I set my cocoa on the small, glass patio table. "Let me get my jacket and a couple of wraps."

Within minutes I returned to the balcony, jacket on, two throws in hand. Adam stood at the railing his back to me. I put his throw in a chair then sat down, spreading my throw over my legs.

Cradling the cocoa in my hands, I sipped while gazing at Adam's profile.

"Thanks." He turned, lifting his cup before walking to the chair. He pulled the chair closer to mine, then, after lifting the throw, sat down. "This stuff is addictive."

"I know. And full of calories."

"With something this good, who's counting? I'm not."

For a breathless moment, I watched him over the rim of my cup. After lowering it to my lap, I stared everywhere but at him. He was too hypnotic. My senses were already on overload. I didn't want to make more of what was taking place, than our original agreement—*stand-in partners for the holidays.* Still, I knew my emotions were already too involved.

"Are we on for the other functions, or have you had enough of me?"

His question and unnerving stare caused my stomach to flip-flop. My hand shook enough that I steadied my cup, running my finger along the rim, anything to occupy my hands.

"Sure, I'm game if you are."

"Good. I didn't want to have to find someone else. I've kinda gotten used to you." He blew out heavily through his mouth then took another sip. "Now that I'm well fortified, you can ask me anything."

"What happened?" I needed answers about Brittney to see if I wanted to go to the next step. That is, if Adam offered more.

"Brittney?"

I nodded. He didn't see me. Instead he was staring off in space.

"She was all glitz and glamour, but shallow, which I didn't see until we dated for a while. But I soon knew she wasn't marriage material."

"Marriage material? What do you mean by that?"

"Pretty much what Lori said earlier at the house. Brittney expected me to put a ring on her finger and keep her in the manner that she was accustomed to—running with the rich and famous. That wasn't me. I like things simple.

"When I realized what she was after, I broke it off. That's when she decided to make a move on Michael."

He shook his head. "I don't know if she thought I'd get jealous and ask her to come back, but whatever it was, I tried my best to warn Michael that she was only using him. He didn't take my warning kindly. We had words. One thing led to another, and before I knew it, we weren't speaking. Brittney and Michael soon became engaged and then married."

I mulled over what he said. "It looks like he wants to make amends."

"Yeah. But you saw how Brittney acted. Her nose was still all out of joint." He rammed his fingers through his wavy hair, his face scrunched up in distaste. "Whether it was Brittney or Michael that caused the riff between him and me, I can't say. But today is the first time he's even acted like he cared."

107

"It's a step in the right direction. Your relationship probably won't ever be like it used to be, but I think at least you'll be able to talk without animosity."

He shook his head. "I'm not so sure. I don't think Brittney will let it happen."

"There is that. What's that old saying … no wrath like a woman scorned? In your case, you scorned and then tried to jeopardize her relationship with Michael. She may never forgive you. Do you still have feelings for her?"

"No!"

His vehement reply had my heart zinging.

"I realize I never did. It's just, I'm afraid that when Brittney realizes Michael can't give her everything she thinks she's entitled to, she'll leave him. If that happens, it'll destroy him." He rubbed the back of his neck.

"Enough about them." He smiled at me. "I know we're not scheduled for dinner tomorrow, but what if I come to church and take you out to lunch?"

I wanted to say yes. I wanted to say no. I wanted to say I'm getting too attached to you and I think we should call this whole thing off.

"Sure. That sounds good." I kicked myself for accepting his dinner date, if that was what it was.

"Tell me something about you I don't already know." He watched me expectantly.

"Like what?"

"Well, for starters, I didn't know you painted. What other hidden talent do you possess?"

I puckered my face in thought.

"I love to travel, but I have little time or money to do much. So in way of compensation, I take short trips around Texas, scouting out little unknown towns and places. I love history and collecting antiques, that sort of thing."

"I already knew about the antiques by all the beautiful old things you have displayed around your apartment. You have eclectic taste. I like it. Have you been collecting long?"

Laughing, I said, "Only since I was six."

Adam looked shocked.

"My mother threw out an old Raggedy Ann that I'd had since I was three. I carried the old thing everywhere and it was falling apart. When she threw out the doll, that's what started my hording and my love of antiques. Now I make myself muck out the closets and drawers twice a year. And to seek out antique shops only if and when I absolutely need something." A little embarrassed, I looked at him.

Though he didn't laugh, I saw the humor in his eyes.

"I think I know a lot less about you than you know about me. So tell me something about you that I don't know." I liked turning the tables on him.

"I love sports."

"That much I learned at my folks' house when you were glued to the TV." I shook my head. "Doesn't count. Come on. Give me something I can sink my teeth in. Something that no one else knows."

He wrinkled his brow. "I've always wanted to play the guitar and sing in front of a live audience." He got this real cute expression. "But I can't hold a tune."

"Oh, surely—"

"No. Seriously, I can't sing a lick." He tried keeping a straight face. "We used to have a dog that every time I started singing, he'd howl. My folks finally made me go outside and take the dog with me anytime I wanted to sing."

"You poor thing," I sputtered out laughing.

"That doesn't sound overly sympathetic." His sparkling, blue eyes were watching me.

"I'm sorry."

"Sure your are. Would you like to know something else that no one else knows?"

"Sure, and I promise not to laugh this time."

"Good, because it's no laughing matter." He paused. "I'm falling in love with you."

Chapter 14

Talk about wiping the laughter from my face. I didn't know what to say. I stared at him, wondering if he'd lost his mind or was joking.

He took my cup from my hands and set it on the table. "Now I've rendered you speechless."

"What do you expect me to say after something like that?"

"How 'bout I like you too. Or sorry, Adam, you're barking up the wrong tree. Or go take a flying leap."

"I'm stunned."

"Is that a good stunned or bad stunned?" He waited for my reply.

How to explain that I thought he'd lost his mind without hurting his feelings.

"There's no way you can know this soon that you're in love with me."

"Oh, but you forget. The Ryder inclination for falling in love comes quickly."

"Are you trying to hold up a family tradition? Or filling a void left by your cousin?" I twisted my hands.

At first his look was stormy, then it change to one I couldn't read. He captured my hands, holding them in his palm, looking at them as if they were precious, something breakable. I was the one ready to break, not my hands.

"Neither." He nailed me with his gorgeous eyes.

"You have to be out of your mind. We barely know each other."

"I didn't think it possible." He shook his head in disbelief. "I'm like all the other Ryder men. I have fallen irrevocably in love with you. And I believe you feel something for me, too, other than friendship." He looked me square in the eyes. "Tell me I'm wrong."

"Adam." His name whooshed out like a prayer. I removed my hands from his because I couldn't think straight with him touching me. "I won't lie. I am attracted to you. What woman wouldn't be? But love? ... I'm not sure love is possible this soon."

His grin couldn't have gotten any bigger than what it was at that moment. "Yes, ... love is possible this soon. Think about it for a moment. We've known each other for over two years."

"You can hardly call passing in the hall saying *Hi, how are you?* as knowing someone."

"Ah, but that's where you're wrong. For a long time I've watched and waited for the right opportunity to speak to you. When you came out on the balcony the other night, it was perfect timing. I know how I feel, and I'm not about to change my mind. But I'll give you time to see my feelings where you're concerned won't change." He stood and held out his hand. "Shall we go inside?"

When I removed my throw, the cool air chilled me to the bone. I was glad to go back inside where it was warmer and where I could see his face instead of shadows. Maybe then I would know he was teasing.

I sat on the couch and folded my legs under me. Adam sat down at the opposite end.

"You're not going to bail now that you know how I feel, are you?"

"No. But you've given me a lot to think about."

"Good. And while you're thinking, make sure you know that I won't change my mind about loving you."

"Adam, I don't …"

He leaned over, touching my lips with his warm finger. "Shhh. Believe." Smiling, he stood. "I'm gonna leave now. Let you get some rest. I'll see you tomorrow?"

"Tomorrow?"

"Ah, you wound me," he teased. "Lunch. I'm taking you out after church, remember?"

I nodded.

"In fact, I can drive you. That way, we won't have to worry about jockeying cars around."

"That won't work. I have to go early. I'm singing on the worship team tomorrow."

"See …"—he shook his head—"there's one more thing I didn't know about you. You sing and I bet beautifully."

His infectious smile had me grinning.

"I'll take you. I don't mind sitting around listening. It'll be fun. And if I get bored, I'll slip out and find me a donut."

"Are you sure? We have to be there at eight."

"Perfect."

He bent down, kissed me on the brow, then smiled. "I would like to do more, but until you are sure about me and my motives"—he wiggled his brows—"I'll restrain myself." He headed for the front door.

I scrambled off the couch to follow him.

Before opening the door, he turned to me. "On second thought, forget about restraint."

He pulled me in his arms and kissed me thoroughly, leaving me breathless.

"I don't know about you, but I'll sleep a whole lot better now, or not." He tweaked my nose, his deep dimples appearing. "Tomorrow, gorgeous."

He stepped out into the hall, his promise and endearment singing in my ears. I slid the door shut, leaned against the cool wood, my hand covering where his lips had just been. An excitement coursed through my body while I relived the experience of his kiss.

A cheerful whistle, at first loud, began to fade into the distance until it was gone.

Adam? Of course, who else would it be? I smiled.

Tomorrow. Tomorrow what? We'll pick up where we left off. We'll act like nothing happened?

All I knew … tomorrow would come too soon for me, yet not fast enough.

Feeling as if my whole world had changed in an instant with his kiss, I slipped away from the door. I was thrilled that Adam said he loved me, yet, I didn't know if my affections for him were as strong.

I put the cups in the sink to soak and then picked up and folded my afghan. When I lifted the throw Adam used, I raised it to my face and breathed in deeply of his clean, woodsy scent. Again I relived the thrill of his lips on mine.

How did I become filled with such contradictions?

I hugged his afghan tight to my chest, wondering what it would be like to belong to Adam.

I liked him well enough, more than I had ever liked any man before. Still, it scared me that he thought he loved me and that I might have a budding love for him. I enjoyed being around him, and like now, missed him terribly when he was gone. *But love?*

He made me feel alive and as if I could conquer the world. Yet, it was also like walking a tight rope between two 60-story buildings. I was extremely afraid if I allowed myself to love him, one misstep would plunge me to instant death.

Chapter 15

A soft knock on my door had my heart beating like a percussionist in a drum line. I was dressed and ready to leave, but not sure I was ready to see Adam after a sleepless night. It had been well after midnight before I fell asleep, and then only to be woken by a dream.

Brittney, her arms crossed, was standing over me scowling.

Adam can't love you. He's incapable of love.

I had a hard time going back to sleep after that.

Shoving the remnants of the dream aside, I grabbed my purse, and then opened the door, smiling.

Adam took my breath away. He wore black jeans and a blue and green plaid shirt that set his eyes off to perfection.

This was one hunk of a guy that nearly had me drooling.

"Hey, beautiful." He leaned in to give me a peck on the cheek.

"Hey yourself." I pulled the door closed. "You sure you want to sit through practice and then the service later. It'll make for a long morning."

He led me to the elevators and punched the button. "Don't worry about me. I'm a big boy. I can take care of myself."

We stepped into the little cube and began descending.

"Yeah, I noticed." I touched the small purple bruise on his cheek. "Does it still hurt?"

His skin felt warm and smooth beneath my fingers. I had drifted over the line from casual-friendly to intimate. I knew better. Yet, it felt so good.

He placed his hand over mine, kissed my palm, and then lowered our hands to his side, intertwining our fingers.

"No." He smiled. "Only my pride for not seeing it coming."

My heart beat erratically as the heat of his touch sent warmth surging through my body. I wasn't sure what I felt was love, but if it wasn't, it sure was a close second.

Sliding into his car, I sat back and relaxed while he drove. I didn't want to be reminded that I needed to make a decision about Adam. I had labeled us as friends, *good friends*. After last night though, I knew it had passed the good friends stage and was much more. How much? I was uncertain.

When we arrived at church I introduced Adam to the worship team. Several of the women gave me knowing looks. The men had to offer up a little friendly razzing, out of earshot of Adam, thankfully.

After practice, I sat down beside Adam. Several people came by and talked with us, and each person gave me *that* look. I didn't try to explain we were only friends because I wasn't sure I believed it any longer myself.

Mom and Dad, when they arrived, spotted us and naturally came over to say hello.

"Adam, so nice to see you again." My father and Adam shook hands.

"Thank you, sir. Same here."

"I'm so glad you came to visit our church again." Mom glanced over at me then back at Adam. "If you don't have plans, we would love to have you come for lunch." Mom, ever playing matchmaker, smiled innocently. "I always put an extra potato in the pot."

"Thanks for the invitation. But, I've made plans with your daughter to take her out to lunch. But I'll take a rain check, if that's ok with you."

"Oh. How nice." Face beaming, Mom gave a knowing nod. "Certainly. Next week, if you don't have plans, I insist that you come with Whitney for Sunday dinner. Thursday was too hectic to really get to know you properly."

Thankfully, Mandy ran up, distracting everyone. She gave Papa and Nana a hug, then me before looking up at Adam, hands on her hips. "Did you bring Eve?"

The grownups chuckled.

Adam stooped to her level. "No. I'm afraid Eve is gone and is never coming back. Sorry."

"Oh." Mandy's little face scrunched up. I could almost see her little brain churning. She cocked her head to the side, and then her expression turned all serious like. "Don't be sad. My doggie ran off. Mommy and daddy found me a new one. Maybe you'll find a new Eve."

Everyone chuckled again.

"Thanks, Mandy. You give me hope." Adam stood, leaning his head close to my ear. "Out of the mouths of babes ... I've found my Eve."

His closeness sent a thrill of anticipation through me. My heart had more say-so power than my head where Adam was concerned.

117

Chapter 16

Sunday afternoon until early evening, Adam entertained me quite nicely.

Lunch at *Gloria's Latin Cuisine* in Uptown was to die for and I ate like a pig.

Once we were sufficiently full, we drove to Clyde Warren Park where we walked by people playing games, children squealing and running around, and other couples like us—hand-in-hand—were enjoying a relaxing stroll. *A couple?* I guess we were.

While we ambled around the park, I knew I could never tire of Adam. He was interesting, funny, and multifaceted. He knew a little bit about everything. And as before, when I talked he listened, really listened, as if my opinion mattered.

When Adam thought we had sufficiently worn off our meal, he took me to *Wild About Harry's* where he proceeded to order a *Junkyard Dog*—a spicy Texas polish dog with jalapenos.

He tried his best to buy me a dog of my choice, but I protested, saying I was still too full.

Once his order was up, nothing would suffice him until I took a bite of, as he put it, his delicious Junkyard Dog. To my regret, the one small bite I took left my mouth on fire and brought tears to my eyes.

Between hoots of laughter, Adam ordered me a cup of vanilla custard, the only thing that seemed to cool down the burning in my mouth.

"Next time, warn me."

He winked. "Next time, we'll share the Chicago Dog. A lot tamer."

"Humph."

After polishing off his hot dog, he ordered a double dip of vanilla with strawberries, pineapples, and bananas for himself.

"Hey, no fair." I tapped my fingers on the table, my lips in a straight line.

"What?" Little wrinkles appeared between his brows.

"You get toppings and I don't?"

He stood. "What kind would you like?"

I shook my head. "No, that's all right. I was just teasing"

"Don't make me pick. You may not like my choices." His eyes sparkled. "Jalapenos?"

"No! Definitely not." I gave him a look of horror. "Fudge, caramel, and almonds."

He took my cup of frozen custard to the counter and came back with it loaded and overflowing.

"Thanks." I gave a sigh of contentment.

"You're not hard to please." His beautiful dimples appeared. "Hmm. If I had known fudge, caramel, and a few nuts would make you happy, I would have done it sooner."

"Chocolate anything makes me happy."

"I'll remember that."

Around dusk, we left *Wild About Harry's,* got in the car and headed for home.

When he walked me to my apartment, he stopped me from opening the door by holding both my hands, looking deep into my eyes.

"I've really enjoyed our day."

"Thank you, Adam, I've enjoyed the day too … except for that bite of the Junkyard Dog."

"I'm sorry." He gave me a sheepish grin. "But it was funny."

I lightly socked his bicep, to which he feigned injury, rubbing the spot, then ruined it by laughing.

"I really am sorry. But you should have seen your face. It was priceless as the red worked its way up your neck into your cheeks. For a minute there, I thought I was going to have to resuscitate you."

I pursed my lips. "Ha, ha, funny."

He leaned in and gave me a kiss. It was light and brief but filled with emotion, and had me spinning.

Pulling back, he looked straight into my eyes. "Today has reinforced what I already knew."

"What's that?"

"I love you, Whitney."

"Adam …" Doubts filled my mind again. How could he really know this quickly?

"Sh." He put a finger to my lips. "Not yet. I want you to think about me. And when you do, I want you to remember I haven't pushed you into a decision. Instead, I am going to woo you until you see that I am the only man you will ever want or need for the rest of your life."

Again, he leaned in, this time he put his arms around me, pulling me up close, and then slowly his head descended.

The anticipation of his kiss made it all the sweeter. And when I was really enjoying the moment, his lips released mine, leaving me with an overwhelming loss.

Still in the circle of his arms, he rested his forehead on mine and breathed in deeply. "You're slowly killing me.

I'm going to miss my Whitney fix while I'm gone this week."

"Gone? Where are you going?"

He didn't move. We remained as we were, arms around each other, foreheads together.

"I'll be down in Houston until Thursday. But I'll call you every night, if that's ok." He pulled back to look at me.

"I'd like that." I knew I would miss him too, but I couldn't bring myself to tell him.

"And, I'll be here on Thursday in time to pick up the salad and pizza and take you to the church."

"You don't have to come or supply pizza."

He growled. "Yes, I do. I want to be with you, even if there will be a crowd."

"Threes a crowd?"

"Yes, when I want to be alone with you."

The seconds ticked by in silence. Again he dipped his head and gave me a sweet kiss. Then just as quickly, he released me and stepped back.

"Go on inside. I'll wait until I know you are safely behind locked doors."

I didn't want to go in, but I knew I should. "Adam, thanks so much for the lovely day. I really enjoyed my time with you."

"Same here." He nodded toward the door. "Go on. Get inside."

"Goodnight."

When the door shut, like last night, I heard whistling fading away until the sound was gone. This time I knew it was Adam.

Already I had an ache in my heart, knowing I couldn't wait until Thursday. Yet, I knew I needed this time to get my head on straight, see if what I felt for Adam was love.

He was everything and more I had dreamed of in a man. Yet love? Could love possibly come this fast and furious? Only time would tell.

I went through the routine of getting ready for bed, all the time thinking of Adam.

Was it only a little over a week since that night on the balcony? I didn't know whether to call it fate or my stupidity that brought us together.

I reached for my cellphone and nearly dropped the thing when it started ringing.

"Hello?" My voice wobbled and my pulse quickened.

"Hi gorgeous."

My adrenaline spiked again at the sound of Adam's chuckle. "Adam? Something wrong?"

"I miss you."

"Oh." *Lame, Whitney, lame. Tell him you miss him too.*

"I turned off the light, and I had this overwhelming desire to hear your voice one last time before I closed my eyes. I hope you weren't asleep."

"I wasn't.

"Good. Well, goodnight, and have pleasant dreams. I know I will."

"Goodnight, Adam. Have a safe trip." The phone went dead. "I'll miss you."

Chapter 17

I was slammed at work. My schedule turned out to be fuller than normal, which wasn't all bad. Less time to dwell on Adam.

When I got home from work, Dad called asking for a family meeting. He wanted all siblings to come for dinner Tuesday night. Though I pressured him to tell me what was up, he said I'd have to wait until tomorrow night. He would tell everyone his news over dinner.

I could hear in his voice he didn't sound right, worried was more like it. But then, not being able to see his face, I couldn't be certain.

Adam called just as I slipped into bed. Hearing his voice thrilled me, but he didn't sound his usual upbeat self either—more tired than anything.

"You sound exhausted. They must be working you hard."

"It's been a rough day. I'm afraid I had to make a few tough decisions that didn't set well. In fact, we're still hashing out the logistics over the deal. I called a fifteen-minute break to slip out and call you. Otherwise, I figured if I didn't do it now, you'd be asleep."

I chuckled. "You figured right. I just hopped into bed."

"I needed to hear your voice." He exhaled heavily. "I miss you."

I only hesitated for a few seconds, and then said what I felt in my heart. "I miss you too."

"Do you really?" He laughed like a giddy teen. "You miss me?"

"Yes, Adam, I miss you." The phone went silent for a moment.

"Aw, Whitney. I can't tell you how that makes me feel."

"I'm sorry things aren't going well. Hopefully, you can get them hammered out quickly. More times than not, a good night's sleep works wonders. And in the light of day, you might see things differently."

"I wish I could take your advice, but the way things are going, we'll probably be here well after midnight." He breathed out wearily. "Enough about me. How did your day go?"

"Too busy."

We continued to talk about trivial things, until someone in the background called Adam's name.

"Thursday can't come fast enough. In fact, I'm going to try to get back into Dallas Wednesday afternoon. I'll give you a call if I do, and if you don't have plans, I want to take you to dinner."

"No plans. And yes, I'd love it, if you get back in time."

"Sleep well. I love you, Whitney."

"Goodnight, Adam."

There was several seconds of silence, as if he were willing me to tell him what he wanted to hear.

"All right then."

I could hear the disappointment in his voice, but I wasn't ready to say the words. It was too soon. I was still too unsure.

"I'll call you tomorrow night. Goodnight."

When he hung up, I couldn't wait until Thursday to see him, or even better, Wednesday if he made it back home in time.

It took a while to go to sleep. Once I did, I dreamed of Adam.

All day Tuesday, my mind was thoroughly occupied by Adam and Dad.

In my mind, I milled over how I felt about Adam.

As much as I didn't want to admit it, and knowing by everyone's standards it was way too soon to tell, I knew I was head over heels in love with him. That is, if being in love meant feeling the wispy wings of butterflies fluttering and taking flight each time he touched or kissed me. Or if feeling like half of me was missing when he wasn't around, then, definitely, I was in love with Adam.

How had it happened … and so quickly?

Where Dad's news was concerned, I speculated all sorts of things. Calling a family meeting generally meant something major was happening. He could be getting a promotion, or maybe even a raise in pay. No, that was out. Dad never discussed financial matters with the family, unless it was dire.

Losing his job? I knew that was impossible. He'd accepted the job with the Metzger Company straight out of college. For over thirty years, he'd worked his way up the ladder and was managing his own team in the company.

I drove straight from work to the house, hoping to get there before my brother and sister, yet knowing I wouldn't.

Sure enough, Seth's and Shelly's cars were both in the drive. The aroma of spaghetti dinner drifted out the door as I walked in.

"Hi Dad. Seth."

Dad looked up from the 6:00 o'clock news and smiled. "Hi sweetie."

After giving him a hug and a kiss on the cheek, I snagged my brother from behind, hugging him, and then ruffling his hair.

He swatted at my hand. "Hey, don't mess with perfection."

I snorted. "You wish."

Their attention was back on the news, but not before I noticed Dad was acting a little out of sorts, like he didn't feel well. "You ok, Dad?"

"As fit as a fiddle." His smile didn't quite reach his eyes.

"Auntie Whitty!" Little Mandy came running from the playroom and wrapped her arms around my legs. She grabbed my hand, tugging. "Come play with me."

I picked her up in my arms, gave her a kiss on the cheek, and then nuzzled her neck. Her immediate response was a squeal as she wiggled and laughed.

"I can't play right now. Maybe after dinner. And I think Nana has supper ready. And you know what?

"What?" Her eyes grew round.

"My smeller tells me"—I sniffed loudly—"Nana's fixed our favorite food."

Her face turned animated. "'ba'sequetti?"

"Yes! I believe you're right. Shall we go see?"

"Uh-huh." Her little head bobbled up and down.

I carried Mandy into the kitchen. "Look who I found? And she's wanting to know if my smeller's right on. Do we smell 'ba'sequetti?"

"Awe." Mom grinned at us. "How did you guess?"

"We were right, Mandy." Mandy and I smacked hands in a high-five.

"'Ba'sequetti." Mandy's little mouth turned round. "Oooo." She wiggled and I put her down.

I walked around to give Mom a hug.

"Hey, sis."

"Hey, yourself." Shelly opened the oven door and peeked inside. "Could you grab that hot pad for me, please."

I handed her the oven mitt. "What can I do?"

Mom blew a wayward strand of hair out of her face. "Take the salad to the table, tell your dad and Seth to wash up, and then come back and help Shelly get the bread in the baskets and glasses to the table."

When everything was done and we were sitting around the table eating, I wondered if Dad would tell us why he called. When he wasn't forth coming, I was on the verge of prompting him.

"What's up Dad? Why the meeting?" Seth shoveled a fork full of spaghetti into his mouth.

"Let's enjoy the meal, and then we'll have our discussion after dinner."

"What's a family-ah-'cussion?" Mandy looked at her papa for the answer.

"It's when someone has something very important to say, and then everyone else talks about it. That's a discussion."

"Oh."

"How's Adam doing?" Mom watched me. "I like him. He seems like a nice man."

I didn't want to talk about Adam. The topic was too personal, especially since I was ninety-nine percent sure I loved him. Still, that one percent of uncertainty was holding me back.

"He's in Houston on business this week." I glanced at Seth and Shelly. "He and his step-sister Lori have volunteered to help this Thursday night."

"Really." Shelly's brows rose, a little know-it-all smile in place. "His sister. How nice."

"Great! That lets me off the hook." Seth grinned.

"I'm afraid not, big brother. I need all the help I can get, including yours." I knew I had an inducement. "Adam's treating us to pizza and a salad, if that makes you feel better."

"Not much. But it helps. I'll be there." He shrugged, already bored with the topic.

"For me too?" Little Mandy looked excited.

"Don't you remember, your mama's dropping you off, and we're having a fancy-dress tea party?" Mom got all animated. "We're wearing hats, gloves, long gowns, and lots and lots of jewelry. And I'm pulling out the fancy plates, tea cups, and saucers."

"Really?" Mandy wore a pure look of delight. "Mama, Nana and me are having tea."

"I heard. That sounds like fun."

"It sure sounds like you're getting hot and heavy with Adam." Seth was wearing his detective look. "Something you'd like to tell us?" He'd finished off his food and was stretching back, his hands locked over his trim belly, his eyes probing.

I smirked, knowing I'd get a rise out of him. "Nothing at this time. But when there is, I'll make sure you hear about it."

"Just what do you know about the man? He could be a serial killer or worse."

I laughed. "Worse? What could be worse than a serial killer."

Seth grunted. "You don't want to know."

"If Adam had a checkered past, you would have already told me. It's for certain, by now you've done a preliminary check to see if he has any outstanding warrants or tickets, or if he's been in jail. My womanly intuition tells me you didn't find a thing." I gave him a challenging stare.

Dad chuckled. "I think she has you there, Son. Give it a rest. Personally, I like the man." He smiled, nodding at me. "Anyone who could put up with Seth and Jed's interrogation and Grandma pulling out all the skeletons from the closet and still wants to stick around, the man is all right in my book."

"Thanks, Dad." I felt like kicking my brother under the table, but refrained from the childish action.

"If everyone is through eating, why don't we move to the living room while we let our dinner settle. We can have dessert later." Dad stood. "It's time to tell you why I asked you to come to the house."

We all moved into the living room. Mandy took that as her cue to run to the playroom.

I didn't like the grave look on Dad's face. The news couldn't be good. The thought frightened me that one of my parents might be deathly ill.

Dad glanced around the room. "Yesterday evening, I received word that my company is in the process of negotiations and will be bought out." He rubbed a hand over his eyes before continuing. "The scuttlebutt around the office is the new owners plan on letting everyone go, including me."

Chapter 18

"Can they do that?" I wanted him to tell me no, his job was safe. I knew better.

"Yes, and the word before I left work this afternoon is they will. The contract was signed today." He tightened his lips. "We haven't received the official word yet. But it's just a matter of time." He looked tired and wrung out.

I wanted to cry, scream, even throw a tantrum.

At fifty-five, Dad was too young for retirement benefits. And at his age, he would be hard put to find a job to fit his qualifications and with his same salary. *Over qualified* is what he would more than likely be told once he started searching for a new position.

Seth leaned down, hands clasped, elbows on his knees. He looked up at Dad worried. "What about your retirement? Is it safe?"

I hadn't thought of that.

He shook his head. "No, I don't think so. I heard the new buyers don't have to honor the retirement agreement. And it appears they will use the capital to pull Metzger out of the hole and save the company."

"They shouldn't have the right to do that." Shelly rubbed her belly, her brow wrinkled. "Isn't there something you can do? Maybe a lawyer?"

"Nothing."

Dad was putting on a good front, but I could see Mom and he were both affected by the devastating blow.

"I don't want any of you to worry. You're mom and I will be okay. We have some savings set aside just for this kind of emergency. And if need be, I can draw from the retirement account I've been setting aside each month until I find another job."

Seth snorted his face scrunched in contempt. "Yeah, and you'll pay huge penalties if you do draw from your retirement." He raked his hand through his hair. "There should be a law against corporate raiders, at least where the retirement packages are concerned. They shouldn't be able to touch that money."

"The only reason I'm telling everyone now, I didn't want you to hear about the sale of the company from some other source. I've started working on my résumé to get it out to the headhunters. I feel confident I won't be out of work for long."

"I'm sure you won't be." This came from Shelly.

We talked more about how he should go about looking for work and the details of what he needed to do next.

By the time I got home, it was already going on ten. I was a little surprised I hadn't heard from Adam yet, but more concerned over my father's news than by Adam's not calling.

I got dressed and crawled into bed, but my mind was on overdrive worrying about my folks. I said my prayers, including asking for a remedy for my father. Grabbing my iPad, I pulled up a book, thinking it might help me go to sleep.

My cellphone rang. It thrilled me to see Adam's name.

"Hey, how are you?"

He laughed. "You don't want to know. It's been a tough couple days. But hearing your voice, I'm already feeling better."

"Well, I'm glad I could make your day."

"You more than make my day."

I wanted to tell him about Dad, but figured he had enough on his plate. And by the sound of it, his day hadn't been much better.

"I'm sorry, but I'm going to have to stay in Houston tomorrow to wind up business here. Can we do dinner Friday night instead of tomorrow night."

"Certainly. And don't worry about picking up pizza on Thursday. "

"No, I've already made the arrangements. And you can ride with me."

"And just exactly where will you put me? In the frunk? You're going to need room to carry the pizzas and salad."

He laughed. "I've got it covered. Gino's delivers. We just have to be there when it arrives."

"Sounds like a plan." It seemed like a lifetime since I'd last seen Adam, instead of only two days.

"I have never missed anyone as much as I've missed you."

"It'll be good to have you back in town."

"You don't know how much. But since it's so late, I won't hold you." He paused. "But when I get back, we need to talk. There's something I need to tell you."

"About what?"

"Not over the phone. I need to see your beautiful face and look into your warm brown eyes."

"My ..." I chuckled, not knowing what to think. "It must be very important."

"It is. But it will hold until I see you again. Maybe after we're finished at the church, we can have some of your famous hot chocolate and talk."

"Sure, that'll work." My mind conjured up all sorts of scenarios, none of them good.

"I'll see you Thursday night. Goodnight. I love you."

"Goodnight." I paused, not able to say the words he wanted to hear. "I miss you, Adam."

"Maybe this trip hasn't been so bad after all." There was a smile in his voice.

"How so?"

"It seems the old saying must be true, … absence makes the heart grow fonder. Goodnight, love."

Chapter 19

Thursday night couldn't come soon enough. Fortunately, during the day I was swamped with work, which made my time fly and kept my mind from counting the hours till Adam's return. I even brought home some work Wednesday night to occupy my evening.

When Adam called Wednesday night, we spoke only briefly. Distracted and not his usual upbeat self, I worried they might be pushing him too hard on his job, but hesitated to say anything. I was so close, but still not ready to step to that next level in our relationship—commitment.

I told myself Adam wasn't like other men, yet one piece of my heart still held the belief he didn't truly know his own mind.

Thursday, I left a little early from work so that I could go by a little boutique in Highlands Village where I liked to shop. I wanted to pick out something special but practical for tonight, since this was a work detail.

Running pretty close to the wire for time to leave for the church, I pulled into the parking garage but didn't see Adam's car.

Since he hadn't called, I figured he was home but like me had gone out to run errands.

I rushed to my apartment, laid out the outfit on the bed, then proceeded to get dressed. Knowing I would be digging in closets and boxes for dusty props and costumes, I would have worn my old blue jeans and an old sweatshirt. Tonight, however, I wanted to look special for Adam.

After removing the tags, I pulled on my new black jeans and the sweet little top with rolled cuffs and little sparkly studs across the front. I twisted before the mirror satisfied I didn't look too bad and didn't look too overdressed either. I swished the brush through my hair, deciding to pull it back at the base of my neck.

Noticing it was 5:30, and since I hadn't heard from Adam, I figured I'd go to his apartment to let him know I was ready. I picked up my purse, grabbed my phone and keys, and headed for the door.

My cell rang. It was Adam.

"Hi, I was just on my way over to your apartment."

"That's why I called. There was a delay at the airport. My flight just landed. As much as I hate the idea, you'll need to go on without me."

"That's ok. I'm sure your exhausted. Don't worry about coming tonight. Lori, Seth, and Shelly are coming. I'll have plenty of help."

"No, I'll be there. Just a little later than planned. I'll get to the church as quick as I can. I've already paid for the pizza and the tip. So when it's delivered, don't wait on me to eat. Just save me a couple of slices and a little salad."

"All right, I'll see you there."

Adam hung up without saying goodbye or even saying he loved me. Disappointed, I chalked it up to him being worn out from all the meetings, the trip, and late arrival.

Being the first to arrive, I opened the door, turned on the lights, and then waited for the pizza delivery person. Through the window I saw a little beat up Toyota pull into

135

the drive and then park. The young man pulled out a warming satchel, several plastic bags, and then looked around.

I opened the door and motioned to him that this was the right place.

After he sat his load on the table I asked, "Do I owe you anything?"

"Nope. Paid in full by"—he looked at the ticket—"Adam Ryder."

"Thanks." I followed him back to the door and noticed that Lori and Shelly had both arrived.

When they entered, Shelly sniffed the air. "Mm, something sure smells good, and I'm starving."

Laughing, I asked, "When are you not starving?"

"I know. Isn't that pitiful." She wrinkled her nose. "Hopefully after this big guy is delivered, I'll be back to normal." She rubbed her belly.

Lori glanced around. "Isn't Adam here? I thought he was coming with you."

"His plane arrived late. He said he'd meet us here and to save him some pizza."

The door flew open and Seth stormed in. His gaze searched the room and then landed on me. "Where is that lowlife?"

"Seth!" My brother wasn't usually that rude and caustic in front of a stranger. I turned to Lori. "I'm sorry. Please excuse my brother. He must have had a bad day." I attempted a smile, not sure what was going on or who he was looking for.

"When you find out what the dirt-bag has done, you'll be as upset as I am."

"Done?" Shelly looked worried. "Who are you talking about? What are you so riled about?"

Once again the door opened. This time Adam walked in. The whole room lit up. I knew right then, I not only missed him, but I loved him.

My brother walked right up to Adam, standing less than a foot away.

"If I weren't the law and knew that you would probably sue the city for my actions, I'd beat you to a pulp." Seth's fists doubled up at his sides, his breaths came in huffs as if he'd already been fighting.

Adam didn't seem surprised by Seth's actions. "Have you told them?"

I rushed over to where they stood, afraid someone was going to get hurt.

Seth's laugh was humorless and frightening. "Maybe you'd like to do the honors." A sneer spread across his mouth.

Pulling at Seth's arm, I asked, "Know what? What's going on?" I looked back and forth from Seth to Adam. I stomped my foot. "Answer me."

Shelly and Lori, standing a few feet away, looked frightened. Shelly anxiously rubbed her belly, while Lori held a trembling hand to her mouth.

The wretched look on Adam's face made me physically ill. I wrapped my arms across my stomach to ward off the fear of what I would hear.

"My company purchased Metzger."

I sucked in a shaky breath, shaking my head, staring in horror at Adam. "No." Tears collected in my eyes as my dreams fell like ashes around my feet.

Adam's countenance pleaded with me to understand as he reached out to touch me. "Please. Let me explain."

Shaking my head, I backed away.

"Whitney, please. I need to—"

Grabbing my purse and jacket, I ran out of the building, the door slamming behind me. The noise effectively cut off Adam's words.

There was nothing he could say that would change what he had done to my father.

I hopped into my car and peeled out of the parking lot. In the review mirror, I saw Adam outside, his hand on the back of his neck, watching me drive off.

Even now, my traitorous heart yearned for him.

Where I was headed, I didn't know. All I knew was I couldn't face my parents. And, I couldn't go back to my apartment where I might run into Adam.

Betrayed. Devastated. My heart was broken.

He said he loved me. But how could he do that to my family if he did?

Why didn't I see this coming? Yet, how would I have known?

Adam had given no sign of what he was capable of doing. On the outside, he was sweet, polite, even considerate of my feelings. Inside, the man was cold, cruel, and heartless. One minute telling me he loved me, the next delivering a death-shattering blow to my family.

I was the one who had brought Adam into their life. I helped destroy their dreams. Me.

Oh, I'm sure, if I'd never made the bargain with Adam, the Metzger deal would have still happened. Yet, I felt to blame, like I'd had a hand in its making.

Tears streamed down my face as I pulled into a parking lot, no plan forming in my head until I looked up. *Target.*

I swiped my eyes and stared at the sign. Then I took a big sniff to clear my clogged nose.

My cell phone rang. *Adam.* I muted the ring and threw the cell back in my purse before sliding out of the car and heading for the store.

The automatic doors opened and warm air swished out, hitting me in the face. I jerked on the handle of a shopping cart before heading in the direction of clothing. Ramming my cart down the aisles like a demented woman on a mission, I rustled through the racks searching for an oversized t-shirt, then a pair of warm-ups. Then I found the underwear, throwing a package of cotton hip-huggers in on the pile of things I had collected. When I finished in the makeup and creams section, I headed for the snack isle.

If I was going to hide out in misery, I might as well pig-out. I grabbed a bunch of snacks, stuffing them into my cart. And to appease my conscience and to show I hadn't completely gone off the wagon, I picked up a banana and an apple, just in case I came to my senses before I gained 10 pounds on this eating binge. I snatched up a large box of extra soft tissues throwing it on top of everything before heading for the checkout.

My shopping cart looked like I was hunkering down for the winter.

The young woman checking me out gave me a smile. "Looks like you're having a party."

A pity party. "Something like that." I slid my ATM card through the device and then entered my number.

"Have a good time."

Nodding, I shoved my cart like a madwoman toward the exit, wanting to make a quick escape before the floodgates opened and I began crying like a baby again.

I drove to the closest motel, checked in, and then plopped on the bed, Throwing one huge crying fit. I railed at Adam, called him several ugly names, then felt guilty for blaming him.

Like me, he had a job to do. But unlike him, I didn't take jobs away, close up companies, leave people destitute. But in all fairness, Dad's company was having issues. Even Dad had said so. But that didn't excuse Adam's part in the demise of my dad's job.

Hearing the message alert on my cell, I picked it up and scanned the missed calls and messages. I had five unanswered calls from Adam, two from Seth, three from Shelly, and two from Dad. I refused to listen to their messages.

The text messages were piling up too.

Adam:	We need to talk. Where are you?
Seth:	I'm sorry. Where are you?
Shelly:	Sis, I'm worried sick. Call me.
Dad:	I know you think it's your fault, but it's not. Everything is ok. Call me. Love Dad.
Adam:	I'm worried about you. Please call. I love you.

Ha! Love.

The man didn't know the meaning of love. If he did he would have … what?

I took a deep breath and in one message texted everyone back except Adam:

| Me: | I'm OK. I need time to think. I'm staying at a motel tonight. Call you tomorrow. |

My text to Adam was short and to the point.

| Me: | I don't want to talk. Don't contact me again. |

I pushed send.

My heart felt like it would explode.

I turned off my phone so I wouldn't be bothered with any more texts or calls. I needed to be alone. Work things out. And hopefully, get over the hurt of Adam's deception.

Maybe I was doomed to be alone. For certain, life would be less complicated … less hassles.

With an unhealthy size of snack wrappers on the floor and the apple and banana staring at me accusingly, I felt more miserable, stomach-wise and emotion-wise, than before I began the junk-food binge. I rolled over, hugging

140

the pillow to me, not wanting to feel anything. I just wanted to sleep and never wake up.

With Adam, I hurt worse than I had ever hurt with any man, including El Jerko Jeremy.

The thought of never seeing Adam again was nearly ripping my heart from my chest. I cried some more, the pain tearing me up inside felt worse than anything I'd ever felt in my entire life.

I wished I had never become involved with Adam Ryder. My traitorous heart reminded me I loved Adam.

I must have dozed off. A loud, awful pounding startled me awake. Disoriented, I shook my head to clear the fog from my brain.

I wasn't home. I was in a motel room. The pounding was coming from my door.

I grabbed the banana, ready to fight off a would-be attacker and then laughed.

A lot of good a banana would do, unless I smushed it in the attacker's eyes, blinding him momentarily.

"Whitney, open the door."

"Seth?"

Even on my tiptoes, the peephole was so high I couldn't look out into the hall to make sure it was my brother.

"Yes, it's me. Open up. We're gathering a crowd out here."

Flipping the little bar back, I pulled open the door, still holding my banana like a gun. "How did you find …" My mouth went dry. Not only was Seth standing there but Adam was too, along with several other motel guests poking their heads out of their rooms, watching.

Adam looked anxious, as he should, but he also looked too good for my faithless heart, which wasn't right.

"What did you hope to do with that banana? Shoot us?" Seth laughed.

At least, Adam had the decency not to smile. He looked miserable and watched me like a starving man.

I felt my cheeks heat up. "I-I-ah-I was going to eat it. Would you like some?" I held it out to my brother.

"No. We're here to take you home."

Glad I hadn't changed my clothes, but knowing I looked all rumpled, I backed up. Using my banana as a pointer, I asked. "Why is he here? I don't want to see him."

I turned around, catching a glimpse of the wrappers strewn across the floor, the bed rumpled, my pillow streaked with mascara, and wanted to crawl under the bed, except there wasn't enough space.

"Didn't you get my message? I want to be left alone."

Knowing I must look a sight, I gave a glance in the mirror over the desk. Black streaks of mascara were under my eyes and on my cheeks. I turned my back, took the edge of my new top, and hurriedly swiped at the gunk under my lashes. Yanking the ponytail holder off, I raked my fingers through my hair that was half in and half out of the holder. Even after doing all that, I didn't look much better.

Pushing the hair from my eyes, I moved over and shoved some of the wrappers under the desk with my foot, then stopped. Who was I trying to impress? Certainly not Adam Ryder. *He's dead to me.*

Chapter 20

The door shut quietly behind both men. The space suddenly became too small for the three of us. Adam, guarded and looking uncertain, came no farther than a few feet inside the room.

Seth moved around the room like he was in search of evidence.

"What were you doing?" He kicked a few wrappers around. "Having a party?"

"No. I didn't have dinner." I gave a quick glance at Adam then back at Seth. "So I had a few snacks."

"A few? Looks like you bought out the snack bar and then proceeded to take on a junk food high." He pulled out the desk chair, straddled it backwards, chuckling. "Adam has something to tell you."

He motioned for Adam to sit down in the only remaining chair in the room.

Folding my arms, I glared at Seth, ignoring Adam completely. "How did you find me?"

Seth grunted. "You're asking me, a decorated police detective? Get real."

"Hmm." I stood my ground still ignoring Adam. "I don't care to hear what he has to say."

"Get down off your high-horse. Sit down, and listen to the man. You just might be interested since it involves Dad."

Huffing, I leaned against the wall, my arms crossed, tapping my foot.

Seth looked over at Adam, giving him a half smirk, shaking his head. "Are sure you want her? At times she can be a royal pain in the backside ... like now."

"I'm sure." Adam's gaze never left me. "Whitney, I came to explain about the Metzger buy-out."

What could he tell me that would change anything?

"To begin with, I didn't know your father was employed at Metzger when we started the proceedings. I found out Wednesday. That's one of the reasons I didn't fly back to Dallas."

"Wise choice," I mumbled.

"Will you just be quiet and give the man a chance?" Seth looked ready to tear into me.

I motioned for Adam to continue.

"When I first learned that Metzger was in trouble, I targeted the company for a buyout and to possibly clean house, if it warrant such. I took a closer look at the employees and the management staff. It's my job to see if there is any chance of salvaging the business and keeping the employees." He ran a hand over his brow, the strain from the last few days showing in his face.

"My boss was all for closing down the plant and offices and selling off the property. However, since this was my deal in the first place, he left it to me to make the call. That is, I had to prove to him in black and white the reason for my choice—whether to keep Metzger open or closed."

He licked his lips. "Wednesday night I did another more in-depth study of the business. I dug deeper to see what, if anything, I could salvage."

"You could have told me when you called."

"I couldn't." He shook his head. "These deals are always under strict mandates of secrecy. I would be in violation of my contract, which would mean my job if I leaked any portion of the deal before it was completed."

"So where does that leave my father and the others?" I sat down on the edge of the bed, unable to look at Adam. Loving him while knowing he'd deceived me was tearing me apart.

"That's just it, Sis. Adam was able to save Metzger. Dad won't lose his job."

I looked from Seth to Adam. "Is that true?"

"Yes." His eyes told me there was something more.

"Yes ... but that's not all of the story, is it?"

"It isn't. I had to let some employees go. Metzger was overstaffed and there had to be cuts. Some employees were fired outright. Others, like your father, were given a choice to either stay at a reduced salary or leave. The deal is healthy. The company will begin to make a profit again. If not, I lose my job." He shrugged.

"Did Dad take your offer?" Hope fluttered in my chest.

"He did."

"And his retirement is saved?"

"It is for now. However, if the company doesn't turn around, your father could be in the same position further down the road." He ran a hand over his brow. "There's no guarantees in life, as you well know."

I thought over what Adam had to say and knew he wasn't to blame. If Metzger was going under, and Dad had mentioned Metzger's trouble a few times in the past, then Adam did a good thing by saving the company and Dad's job.

"Now that you know the story, where does that leave us?"

Seth stood and stretched. "I believe that's my cue to go get a Coke so you two can iron out your differences. While

I'm gone, I'll let the folks and Shelly know you're ok." He looked sheepishly at me. "And Sis, if you want my opinion, you better listen to your heart." He nodded in Adam's direction and then headed out the door. "I'll be back in ten."

My brother made sure he slid the safety lock in place so the door wouldn't close completely. The clunk sounded loud in the quiet room.

Adam didn't move, just glanced around. "Did you really eat all that junk?" He waved his hand at wrappers under the desk and scattered across the floor, furrows etched deep between his raised brow.

"Afraid so." I offered a shamefaced grin.

His laughter filled the room and my heart.

Holding out the bruised-looking banana, I said, "I do have a banana if you're hungry. Or an apple?" I pointed at the shiny fruit on the nightstand.

He shook his head. "Only you would offer me something to eat when we need to have a serious conversation in less than"—he looked at his watch—"eight minutes before your brother is back ready to haul you out of here."

After setting down the banana, I glanced at Adam as I chewed on my bottom lip

"Are you going to answer my question?"

Adam's stare went through me like a hot searing iron.

"I'm sorry I jumped to conclusions. I should have given you a chance to explain." I grimaced. "I'm afraid sometimes I have a tendency to leap without all the facts." Again I began chewing on my bottom lip. "But I've been working on that flaw. And I'm getting a little better at it, if you don't count tonight."

"You still haven't answered my question." His serious demeanor made me nervous.

"If you'll forgive my lapse in judgment—"

"Trust. Your lapse ... was more an issue of trust."

146

"Yes, you are correct. And for that I'm sorry."

Without a doubt, I didn't want to lose Adam. He meant too much to me.

I took a deep breath before continuing, "I'd like to begin where we left off before I thought I had all the answers. If that makes sense." I resisted the urge to touch him.

Shaking his head in disbelief, he chuckled. "Believe it or not, your words make perfect sense. I guess that mean's I'm beginning to understand you."

"Adam, I don't know what to say, except I'm truly sorry. Will you forgive me?"

"You're forgiven. But—"

"There's that *but* factor." I drugged my bottom lip through my teeth.

"In order for us to get married—"

"Married?"

"Don't interrupt."

I closed my mouth.

He still wants me.

"Like I was saying, if we are going to get married, from now on, you're going to have to trust me, or the deal's off."

I snapped my fingers while my body was on Adam alert. "Just like that, we're getting married?" I marveled that Adam was so forgiving.

"Yes. I believe Grandpa Ryder already clued you in how we Ryder men are about our women."

"Women?" Doing my best to keep a straight face, I said, "Are you telling me you have more than one?"

"No, I couldn't handle more than one. You're woman enough for me." His dimples appeared as he shook his head. "I still marvel that Jeremy had the guts and stamina enough for four."

I burst out laughing. "He had his hands full juggling schedules. Even slipped up once and called me Fran."

"He must have had some serious screws loose to let a prize like you get away. But I'm glad he did. So it's settled then … you'll marry me?"

"I don't believe you've asked, or did I miss that part?" I cocked my head to one side stringing him along.

He moved off the chair, bent on one knee in front of me, taking my hand.

At that moment, I realized how much I almost lost. To think my own stupidity nearly cost me this wonderful man, shook me to the core.

I knew what Adam was about to do. My heart beat so fast I could hardly catch my breath. He gazed into my eyes. His were filled with love and desire. I knew if I had let Adam get away, I would miss a lifetime of happiness filled with love.

"Whitney, I love you with all my heart. And I don't say this lightly. I will love you like no man has ever loved a woman. My heart aches for you. Will you marry me?"

Tears filled my eyes, tightening my throat, choking off my answer as I nestled his words away in my heart.

"For Pete's sake, tell the man yes and put him out of his misery."

Seth stood in the doorway, a can of pop in his hand, a silly grin in place.

I nodded. "Yes. A thousand times yes."

"Yes?" Adam looked incredulous. "Did you say yes?"

"Yes, I love you and I will marry you."

He stood, pulling me in the circle of his arms, and then glanced back at Seth. "I'm about to kiss Whitney, so please keep your ankle gun holstered, because I don't want to be shot in the process."

"Keep it short and quick, or you just might find yourself in handcuffs." Seth chuckled under his breath.

Adam tipped his head toward me, melding his lips to mine. The kiss, though gentle was thorough, causing a thrill to surge through my veins. My heart nearly thumped out of my chest to think this incredible man belonged to me.

Seth cleared his throat, causing Adam to lean back, but still holding me in his arms.

The kiss had ended way too soon. Yet, I could still feel the imprint of his lips as if they were still there.

"I love you." He leaned in and whispered in my ear. "And I can't wait to make you mine."

When he pulled by his eyes were dancing.

"I love you too."

"Well, it's about time." Seth grunted from the doorway. "So, let's get this two-ringed circus on the road. Pack your things. I want to get out of here so I can get home and to bed."

It only took me a few minutes to put what little stuff I had left in the plastic shopping bags. When we got out to the parking lot, I saw Seth's car, but not Adams.

"I'll follow you home, Sis."

"Where's you car, Adam?"

He chuckled. "It's back at the church. When we came to find you, Seth thought it best if I rode with him."

"I get the picture."

My brother stood there, arms crossed, his detective face in place. He knew me well enough to know I wouldn't have given Adam the time of day. Yet, acting the big brother, he also didn't want to take the chance I'd let him into my room alone.

"Since you have an early morning at the precinct, why don't you go on home. I'll drive Adam to his car." Spending a little more time with Adam would do me a world of good.

"I don't go to work any earlier than you do," Seth pushed back at me.

"I'm not going into work tomorrow—I called in a sick day." When both guys looked at me oddly I shrugged. "Well ... I was sick at the time."

"I just bet you were." Seth chuckled as he turned to Adam. "She can be a real handful. Are you sure you can handle her?"

"I believe I can." Adam squeezed me up tight.

Seth clapped Adam on the back. "Well, then, I guess congratulations are in order. Welcome to the family."

"Thanks."

He scratched his chin, giving Adam a stern-eyed squint. "Once you've picked up your car, you will follow her home."

"I'd already planned on it."

"Once you're there, make sure she goes straight to her apartment and you to yours."

"Where do you get off telling me what to do? I'm a grown woman, perfectly capable of handling my own affairs."

"Since I became a cop. No, come to think of it, since you were running around in diapers." He laughed, his gaze back on Adam. "You take care of my little sister, or you'll answer to me."

He gave me a hug and a kiss on the cheek, and then got into his car, waiting until we left the parking lot.

"I'm sure Seth will probably spill our news, but I'd still like for us to go together to your folks' house and ask their blessing."

"Adam, are you completely sure about this whole marriage thing? We barely know one another. I don't know what you like to eat. What your favorite color is. How you spend your day. What if—"

He placed a gentle finger across my lips.

"Sh. Listen to me. No more *what ifs.*" His hand fell away. "My favorite color is green. I don't think there is anything I don't like to eat. And just thinking about you turns me inside out. I've never been more sure of anything in all my life than wanting to marry you. We will have a lifetime to learn our likes and dislikes, and we can make up a few new ones as we go along."

He ran his hand along my arm, my body turning warm beneath his touch.

"Do you love me?"

"Yes, I love you."

A cute little grin appeared. "Then that settles that. I don't want to hear any more talk about what if. And now, the only question left is when?"

"When?" I gave a quick glance his way and then back on the road. I knew I loved Adam with all my heart and soul. If for no other reason than it nearly killed me when I thought I had lost him over my father's job. He was everything and more that I wanted in a man, so why the hesitation?

"Yes, when? A Christmas wedding with all the holiday decorations would make for a beautiful ceremony."

"I agree, but isn't it a little too soon?"

I could feel Adam's penetrating gaze searing a path into my mind to find my hesitancy.

"Is there a reason for your reluctance to set a date?"

"But you don't really know me. Like what I did tonight. Well, I guess technically it was last night since it's one a.m., but you know what I mean. What if you … if you learn all my flaws and find you don't like what you see? What then?"

When would I ever get over this fear that Adam would one day look at me and not like what he saw and then dump me for someone prettier, smarter, and more sophisticated?

"Do you snore?"

"No. Or at least I don't think I do."

"Wrestle and squirm in bed?" He quirked his brow, his dimples barely showing. "Well, come to think on it, the wrestling and squirming part would be fun."

I was thankful for the shadows that made it impossible for him to see my scarlet face. Pulling into the church parking lot, I parked my car next to his.

"How 'bout hogging covers. If you do, that just might be a deal breaker." His seatbelt unsnapped

I slapped him on the arm. "I don't hog covers."

He unsnapped my seatbelt. "Come here, you."

Leaning in my direction, he snagged my left shoulder, turning me, pulling me toward him, until only a small gap separated us. He placed his knuckle under my chin and lifted. Our eyes met, and for a brief moment our gaze locked, our breaths mingling.

"Whitney, my love, you could never do or say anything to turn me off, outside of saying you don't love me. Even then, I wouldn't believe you. I would work hard to prove your words false while I showed you all the love I feel for you."

He dipped his head. His warm, undemanding lips dispelled all my objections and fears. As he deepened the kiss, my apprehensions scattered to the winds, knowing Adam would never let me down.

By the time he pulled back, I wasn't sure if I knew my own name, let alone know how to drive home. Adam had stormed the walls of my doubts, broken the chains that held me back, and irrevocably conquered all my fears.

"I love you. And I think a Christmas wedding will be great!"

Adam let out a whoop that filled the car. "Yes! I can't tell you how happy you've made me." A gorgeous grin, dimples and all, appeared. "But I sure can try to show you."

The first kiss was awesome? The second one was even better. But the last kiss rocked my world down to the very core of my being, leaving no room for doubts.

Chapter 21

What have I done? What was I thinking?

In the light of day, my reasoning seemed flawed. My quandary wasn't that I loved Adam. There was no debate about that.

My predicament was how would I plan a wedding in less than three weeks. I had four Christmas parties, two banquets, and several family gatherings to attend. Goodness, I hadn't even put my Christmas tree up yet.

Impossible!

I had to be out of my ever-lovin' mind. By the time the New Year rolled around, I'd be in bedlam for sure.

Oh, no. I forgot about the children's play. How could I? The church and the children were depending on me. It would have to be spliced in somewhere along with everything else.

I lowered my head to my hands, my piece of toast barely touched, my mind whirling with the impossibilities.

Talk about overextended. My only hope was to enlist help.

Lori and Shelly. That is, if Shelly didn't have her baby when I told her our news.

Last night Adam had mentioned it would be nice to have both parents present when we told them our wedding plans for December 26th. He was going to try to arrange dinner with them for tonight, if at all possible.

I needed a new dress for tonight. Something casual, yet dressy, something that reeked of confidence and said I knew what I was doing and had full command of the situation.

I wondered if I could find a dress made of chainmail? I started laughing.

Knowing how totally unproductive it was to go shopping, I didn't care. What was a couple of hours in the grand scheme of things going to matter? After all, I had exactly 23 days, including Christmas and Sundays, until my wedding day. A piece of cake!

My stomach did a somersault. What little breakfast I'd eaten was on the verge of coming up.

Think positive. Make this shopping spree a time for fun. A chance to see what is out there in the way of a simple wedding dress and other items I'll need.

I picked up my phone and punched in Tiffany Ainsley's number, hoping against hope she'd be free.

"Hi Whitney, what's up?"

"Believe it or not, I'm getting married and I need help." I tried to keep the panic from my voice.

"You've got to be kidding. We are invited, aren't we?"

"Of course. But right now I need your expertise since you went through this not too long ago. I have only three weeks to make this happen."

"Oh, my." She laughed. "You believe in doing things fast. What can I do?"

"You wouldn't by any chance have today free, would you?" I grimaced, hoping she would.

"For you, I'll make time. What do you have in mind?"

"I need you to go shopping with me."

"Sure. I'll let Matt know what I'm doing, and then swing by your place to pick you up, say ... thirty minutes?"

"Thank you. That'll work. Call me when you're a couple of blocks away and I'll meet you out front."

Excited about seeing Tiffany, and doing my best not to let panic set in, I made up a list of what I needed to accomplish within the next five hours.

The phone rang and I prayed it wasn't Tiffany calling to cancel.

"Hey, gorgeous."

My heart accelerated when I heard Adam's voice.

"I thought I'd let you know everything is a go for tonight. And ..."

"And what?" I didn't need problems.

"I needed my fix for the morning to hold me over until I see you tonight."

"Now I'm your fix. Kinda like a junkie?"

"It's worse than any junkie. I've got it bad. I'd shrivel up and die if I couldn't hear, see, or touch you."

His words warmed me deep inside.

"What are you up to since you're playing hooky today?"

"I'm going shopping with my friend, Tiffany Ainsley."

"Matt Ainsley's wife?" He sounded incredulous.

"Yes. Do you know them?"

"Sure do. Small world." He chuckled. "Matt and I met a few years back when I bought a company he was interested in. Odd thing, though, instead of making us mortal enemies, we became good friends."

"That's good, because Tiffany is one of my best friends. You'll probably be seeing her often over the next few weeks."

"We should call them and set up dinner one night."

"That would be fun, but we'll do it after the wedding. I have too much to do with little time to do it."

"Don't stress. I'll help you in the evenings. What are you going shopping for?"

"A dress for tonight. And since Tiffany got married last year, she's going along to take me to some places where I could shop for my wedding trousseau."

"Wedding trousseau. I like the sound of that. December 26th can't come soon enough."

The thought of Adam and marriage had my blood racing. "Oh, Adam. I have so much to do between now and then, it makes my head crazy."

"Tomorrow, you will have my undivided attention to do whatever is necessary to help you get things done for the wedding. Make a list, and I'll make it happen."

I heaved a heavy sigh. "I wish it were that simple. But I'll make up a list after we get home from dinner with the folks."

"That's my girl. One step at a time. Listen, I've got to run. But have fun with Tiffany, and tell her hi for me. And don't forget … I love you."

"I love you too." The words slipped out as easily as breathing. "And, Adam …"

"Yes."

"Thanks, your call made my day too."

***

By the time I got back from shopping, I was running up to the wire to get dressed for dinner. I had found a rose-colored form fitting knit dress with a flared skirt, hoping Adam would like how it looked on me.

Funny how I worried more about what Adam would think. Yet, I wanted to please him, make him proud so he would know how much I loved him.

After slipping on my knee-high boots, I twisted back and forth in front of the mirror, my hair swishing around my shoulders, the shirt swaying around my hips like one of those models. Satisfied, I applied the new lipstick that matched the color of my dress and smushed my lips together.

Knowing we needed to leave if we were to arrive at the restaurant before the others, I grabbed my purse and headed out of the apartment. As the door shut behind me, Adam's door opened and out walked Brittney, all smiles.

That little green monster took hold of me. I wanted to rip that smile right off her perfect face. What was she doing in Adam's apartment anyway? And where was her husband?

When she saw me standing in the hall, she hiked a brow, and then without a word slinked like a model across the hall to the elevator. One long, elegant finger with a red-painted nail pushed the elevator button.

She was going to ignore me completely.

I wasn't about to let her. I moved quickly in her direction. "Hi Brittney."

"Oh, that was you, wasn't it?" She didn't seem a bit surprised.

"Yup, me in the flesh." I hoped my smile didn't look as forced as it felt. "How have you been?"

"Fine."

"And your husband, Michael? I hope he's well."

"I wouldn't know. I haven't seen him since Tuesday. He's off on business. That's why I was here visiting Adam."

Hmm. As Grams would say, something smelled rotten in Denmark. Husband out of town and she's here visiting her ex. That didn't set well with me.

The elevator door opened and so did Adam's apartment door. Out stepped Adam. Brittney moved into the elevator, the door closing behind her.

He gave me an appreciative once over, then a wolf whistle. "Wow, you are a knockout in that dress."

I appreciated the whistle and the compliment, but I was still a little ticked off at Brittney being in his apartment without knowing the reason for her being there.

"Are you ready to go then?"

"Ah-yeah. What was Brittney doing here without Michael?"

He shrugged. "She came to ask a favor." He pulled me up close. "Seems she wants to have a surprise birthday party for Michael and needed my help."

"Oh?"

His dimples appeared. "That was my exact word. Then I proceeded to tell her I was getting married, and my time was all tied up with my fiancée." He waited for his words to sink in.

"You did?"

"Yes, ma'am. You want to know something else?"

I nodded as he circled his arms around me and began nuzzling my neck.

Unable to speak while the delicious feelings of his nibbling coursed through my body, I pushed all thoughts of Brittney out of my head.

"I think she accomplished her goal."

"Her goal? What was that?"

"To make you jealous." He looked at me. "Did it work?"

"A little."

He cocked his brow.

"Well, maybe a whole lot. But not anymore."

"Good, because you want to know something else?"

I couldn't answer because he was nibbling my earlobe this time, his breath tickling my neck, sending my senses reeling.

Pulling back, I saw the sparkle in his eyes.

"I love you to distraction. So I hope you know once and for all, no one else will ever be able to replace you in my heart."

Chapter 22

The closer we got to the restaurant, the more anxious I became. What if his parents weren't in favor of the match? Worse yet, what if mine weren't?

Adam hooked my chin, turning my head to look at him.

"If you don't stop chewing your lower lip, there'll be nothing left for me to nibble on."

Adam's teasing glint made me laugh. "You weren't having any problem finding something to nibble while we were in the hall waiting on the elevator."

"True. But I love to kiss you too."

I snorted, then picked at my cuticle with my nail.

He placed his free hand over mine. "Stop worrying."

"Easy for you to say." I rolled my eyes. "What if—"

"We've gone over this. And because I love you, we will go over it again." He pushed down the turn signal, then maneuvered the turn. "*What ifs* don't figure into the equation. All that matters is I love you, you love me, and we're getting married December 26. Tonight is merely a formality, a courtesy to give them the opportunity to jump onboard with the plan." His dimples showed. "But you wait and see. They'll all be happy."

"Easy for you to say." I wanted everyone to be overjoyed, but I was afraid my Dad might still think unkindly of Adam and his company even if he still had his job.

We stopped in front of the entrance of the restaurant. A valet opened my door. When I got out of the car, I waited nervously for Adam on the sidewalk.

Just before we stepped inside, he leaned near my ear.

"I love you."

"I love you too. But my stomach is still tied up in knots."

He tweaked my nose, a scheming look in his eyes. "If I kissed you right here and now, would that take your mind off what's waiting inside?"

Not waiting for my answer, he bent, captured my lips, sending my senses over-the-top crazy.

"All that succeeded in doing was to make my knees weak and my heart race."

"Good." He opened the door, his hand resting on my waist, leading me into the building. "At least I know my kiss still affects you."

"Oh, you can certainly say that."

We followed the maître d' to a corner table next to the window overlooking a courtyard. Jim and Audrey were already seated and waiting. Jim stood as we approached. Audrey sat there positively beaming at us.

"Whitney, so glad to see you again." Jim bent and gave me a hug and then turned to his son. "Tell me this is what I think it is." Jim's eyes sparkled.

Adam hugged his father. "All in due time."

Before I could be seated, the maître d' brought my parents to the table. After introductions and hugs, everyone took their seats.

"By now, I believe you have surmised the reason for dinner with Whitney and me." Adam held my hand under the table glancing in my parents' direction. "First off, I want you to know that Whitney and I are in love, and I would like your permission to marry your daughter."

My father's raised brow didn't bode well for our announcement. But my mother was all smiles.

"Isn't this kind of sudden?" Dad's narrowed-eyed stare made the knots in my stomach dissolve into stinging hornets.

"Not really. May I call you Don?"

He nodded while everyone else at the table watched the scene play out.

Adam squeezed my hand for reassurance, reassurance that at the moment was in short supply. I felt helpless.

"Don, I've known your daughter for the last two years. And though it's true, we've only been dating for a short while, I know enough about Whitney to recognize I want her as my wife and the mother of our children, if we are blessed to have any." Adam smiled over at me, love shining from his eyes. "So I'm asking yours and Addie's permission to marry your daughter."

Silence seemed to ricochet around the table. When Dad didn't say anything, I spoke up.

"Dad, Mom, I love Adam. We have made plans to get married on December 26, and we would like your blessing." My hand shook inside Adam's hand as a collective gasp sounded and I watched the shock of my words.

Everyone except my father was congratulating us.

I turned to my father. "Dad?"

He nodded, sticking his hand out to Adam, a huge smile in place. "Permission granted. But you better make sure you treat my daughter right, because if you don't … you will answer to me and her brother."

"I will, sir."

161

Adam leaned in. "I told you not to worry."

"For a minute there, it was touch and go." I muttered back.

"True." He pulled a small box from his jacket and opened it. A princess cut diamond, with smaller diamonds trailing off on each side, sparkled up at me.

"Awe, Adam. It's beautiful." My gasp drew everyone's attention.

He lifted my left hand. "Whitney, I love you with my whole heart and will until I die. Thank you for accepting my proposal. I will do my best to make you happy."

"You already do." Tears collected on my lashes, blurring my vision as he slipped the ring on my finger.

"I hope you like it. If you don't, we can exchange it for another." He watched me closely.

"I don't want another ring. This one is perfect."

Adam visibly relaxed. "Good." He gave me a quick peck on the lips.

"Let us see." My mother craned her neck, wiggling her fingers at me like an enthusiastic little girl.

Self-consciously, I held out my hand as both women oohed and aahed.

Dad turned to Adam. "Well done."

All my doubts as to whether he had accepted Adam vanished.

"Oh, my! Adam you have excellent taste." Mom's excitement was contagious.

"Yes, you made an marvelous choice." Audrey looked thoroughly impressed.

I couldn't stop looking at the brilliant diamond winking at me. I knew I had gotten the best of the bargain when God blessed me with Adam.

The rest of the evening was filled with wedding questions and plans. *Where were we having the wedding? What about the reception? Did we have our announcements yet? What about a dress? Bridesmaids' dresses? The tuxes?"*

At first, the 26th of December seemed to present a problem to both mothers. Yet, after much discussion, Mom and Audrey agreed, it would take some doing, but they would both work with me to make it happen.

Adam sat back smugly watching. He cocked a brow in my direction, as if to say, *I told you so.*

I pinched his leg and then smiled when he jerked and bumped his knee into the table, rattling the dishes. He took hold of my hand to insure I didn't pinch him again.

The topic was divided into two—the men discussing all manner of men things and the women discussing the wedding plans.

When I mentioned to Audrey and Mom that Tiffany had taken me to a place where I thought I had found a dress that would be just right for our wedding, they put their heads together.

"Your whole day will have to be free tomorrow." Mom's matter-a-fact attitude had me smiling.

"I have some work, but it can wait."

"Good. Because Audrey and I will be at your apartment at 9:30 tomorrow morning." Mom was on a roll. "We'll go to the boutique where Tiffany took you. Hopefully they'll have the bridesmaids' dresses so we won't have to go elsewhere. And maybe the mothers' dresses too." She nodded at Audrey.

"Yes, that would be great if they did." Audrey was writing furiously on a small purse tablet. She looked up at me. "Tonight when you get home, make up a list of things for the wedding, and your mother and I will do the same. We'll compare and cross off duplicates. That way, between the three lists, we will have covered everything you'll need to pull this off."

"A brilliant idea." My mother was quite pleased with her new friend's suggestion.

I smiled, thankful Mom and Audrey had become fast friends. Otherwise, this could have turned out to be a total disaster.

By the time we left the restaurant, I was ready to call it a night. The emotional strain of the evening had taken its toll on me. The two mothers on steroids had my head swimming with all there was to do.

"I'm all for running off and getting married." Adam looked over at me. The streetlights flashed across the planes of his serious face, a face I was coming to love more and more with each passing moment.

"Sounds like a plan, but I don't think we can."

"Sure we can. I'll buy the tickets. Just say the word."

"And have both families disown us? No thank you."

He laughed. "Ah, you're a spoilsport. But I guess you're right."

"Adam."

"Hmm?"

"Are we doing the right thing?"

"Right thing?" His jaw tightened slightly. "Are you having second thoughts that you love me, or that you want to marry me?"

"No, neither. But …"

"Listen, if you'd rather have a large wedding with all the trimmings, I get that. And if that is truly your heart's desire, then I'll go along with it, as long as it isn't six months down the road. But I'll give you three. However, my practical side would rather spend the money on a down payment for a house."

"A house?" The possibilities of our first home together were mind-boggling.

"Yes. I thought after the honeymoon, we would come back and start looking."

"Honeymoon? Have you already planned one?" I was astounded that Adam was thinking so far ahead. First the ring tonight—I glanced down at my finger, the diamond brilliant in the nightlights—and now he'd thought of a honeymoon.

He nodded, "Of course."

"Where?"

"I was going to keep it a surprise, but if you really want to know ... Think soft, tropical breeze, warm, sunny beaches, and—"

"Mm, that sounds heavenly. But on second thought, don't tell me. I want it to be a surprise." I leaned back, closing my eyes finally giving into the tiredness from all the stress. "I don't know how I'll get through the next three weeks. All I have to say is you better have a whole lot of spare time on your hands because I'll be needing your help."

"Babe, whatever you need, I'll move heaven and earth to make it happen."

I chuckled, loving his endearment, and the part of moving heaven and earth. "I'd like to see that."

After Pulling into the underground parking, Adam drove in and parked the car. He turned toward me, taking hold of my hand.

Wondering why he wasn't getting out, I stared at him.

"I was so proud of you tonight when you spoke up to your dad. It took courage and love." He leaned over and gave me a kiss. "Thank you."

Adam's kisses were never ho-hum. Each time our lips touched, my world tipped on its axis, spinning out of control. At the moment, I was glad I was still sitting in the car because I felt like a sailor coming ashore unable to find his sea legs.

How did I become so blessed?

The prospects of a lifetime of love with this man made me ecstatic. I didn't think I could love him more, but each time we were together proved my theory wrong.

Chapter 23

My Saturday shopping spree with Mom and Audrey at Patsy's Bridal Boutique took care of my bridal ensemble. Both women fell in love with the dress I had picked out while shopping with Tiffany. It was a long, formfitting sequin and pearl dress that flared out at the knees, with a sweeping mini train at the back.

Since we were using the green and red Christmas decorations already in place at the church, I chose a candy-apple red satin dress for the bridesmaids. The dresses had an empire waist and a demi jacket with white fur around the neck and sleeves. Thankfully, the seamstress said she would be able to add material to accommodate Shelly's blossoming figure. I bought extra material for Mom to sew Mandy's flower girl's dress to match the bridesmaids.

The bridal boutique also carried tuxedos for the men and Adam's little six-year-old cousin Brandon who would be the ring bearer. I was amazed how much we had accomplished in one day. There was a long litany of things still to be done.

Somehow the list of invitees organically grew with help from both women until I put a stop to it. After I explained to Mom and Audrey we had to be realistic and only relatives and very close friends could be invited, we settled on 200 guests. I was satisfied. More invitations than I had planned on sending, yet, I knew only a portion of the invitees would attend.

Fortunately, I was able to pick up the invitations on Wednesday. I commandeered Lori and Shelly to help me address and stuff the invitations. My brother Seth showed up to help put the stamps on the envelopes, which surprised me.

He and Adam talked and joked around while they worked. Several times, I saw Seth staring at Lori, and then he'd disgruntled and glance away. Not sure what was up with that, and since I didn't have time to bother to find out, I let it go without saying anything.

The days came and went in a blur. By the time I dropped into bed at night I was exhausted and brain dead.

Adam was a great help. Even though we talked several times throughout the day, he would call me on the way home from work.

The nights we didn't have a Christmas function to attend he'd bring home take out or we'd go to a restaurant to eat. From the beginning, he said I had enough to do and didn't need to add cooking and clean up to my long list.

Except for Adam going home to his apartment at the end of each night, we operated like an old married couple. We'd settled into a comfortable routine of going to dinner, pouring over the list, settling disputes, and smoothing ruffled feathers. I enjoyed his company and loved the stolen kisses he'd extracted for a job well done—his not mine.

We booked the church for the 26th, along with the family hall, which was more than ample for our reception. With a few calls, I was able to check the church, musicians, soloist, and minister off my list, which was a load off my mind.

Each night, while working on *the list*, we discussed our future and learned more about each other. Adam said he wanted as many kids as I wanted to give him. Or if it worked out otherwise, we would adopt.

Too many times to count, he mentioned all of the preparations wouldn't be necessary if I would agree to run off with him.

I was beginning to wish we had, but I didn't tell him for fear I would be persuaded.

Everything was falling into place except for Shelly baulking over being my matron of honor. She said she was too huge to waddle down the aisle, and would probably fall or start labor and ruin the wedding.

When I asked if we could change the wedding for the month after Shelly had the baby, Adam put his foot down and adamantly said *no*. When I burst into tears, he pulled me in his arms and comforted me, saying not to worry. He would take care of the matter.

Shelly called the next day and told me she would be in the wedding. I burst out crying again. I seemed to be doing that a lot here lately—stress maybe? When I asked her why she changed her mind, she said Adam had talked with her and she was cool with her duties.

We attended a taste night with the caterers. Adam and I sampled food until I was almost sick. Adam? ... the sampling didn't seem to faze him.

Since we were having an early afternoon wedding, we decided upon sliced beef on miniature buns and sliced turkey on croissants along with salad, pasta, and fruit. My cake ... Italian Cream. And his ... Chocolate Ganache topped with chocolate dipped strawberries.

He was a real sport when it came to the children's Christmas pageant and all the time I had to invest in pulling it together. The night of the dress rehearsal, he adjusted costumes, helped kids with their lines, even straightened halos and angels' wings. When two little shepherds decided

168

to use their shepherd's staff as dueling sticks, he was the one who got them to settle down.

Once little Mandy realized Adam didn't come with an Eve and wasn't the same man who was in the Bible, she fell in love with him. She was over the top when she found out he would be her uncle and she would be in our wedding, wearing a fancy, long dress. It took some doing and several tries for her to understand she wouldn't be throwing petals at the people, just dropping them on the carpet. *What fun was in that?*

With everything falling into place so nicely, I couldn't help but wonder when that old legendary hammer was going to drop and cause a dent in all my plans.

My Christmas banquet was a total success. Adam mingled with the donors, speaking about the success of the charity. His knowledge of the Children's Hospital and what my company did for them surprised.

My boss loved Adam. They were on first name basis, which was another shock since Stan Pinkerton was always addressed as Mr. Pinkerton. And shock No. 2, he also asked for an invitation to our wedding. When I assured him he was on the list of invitees, he beamed at me and said he and his wife would be there.

When it came to Adam's Christmas party ... well all I can say is if I were the jealous type, which I'm not ... *much*, I would have snatched several women baldheaded and Adam would have been bailing me out of jail.

His company seemed to be filled with beautiful, young women who made a point to come by and say hi and give him a close up hug while giving me a narrow-eyed once over. No doubt, they wondered how I was able to get Adam to fall in love with me. I felt like telling them, it was a wonder to me too, but glad he did.

One woman, Cynthia, bolder than the rest, came up and latched herself onto Adam like an octopus. If he hadn't turned his head at the last second, she would have planted her cherry-red lips smack-dab on his mouth and not his cheek. To say she'd taken advantage of the party's open bar was putting it mildly. She was stinkin' drunk.

Adam pried her arms loose, as she looked at him like a besotted teenager.

"Cynthia, allow me to introduce my fiancée, Whitney Singleton. Whitney this is Cynthia Powell, who works in accounting, and at the moment seems to be overly intoxicated."

Cynthia started crying. "Yuz never told me yuz were ge-getting married." She sniffed loudly.

I pulled a tissue from my purse and handed it to the poor woman, impossible not to feel sorry for her.

"Thhank yuz." She blew loudly and then began crying again.

Adam shook his head, then nodded for me to follow. He led her by the arm off to the side of the room, then gently shoved her down in a chair. He motioned for a waiter while Cynthia continued to blubber about how all the good men were taken.

Adam spoke to the waiter and then he turned to Cynthia, who was swaying back and forth in the chair.

"Cynthia, look at me."

She blinked several times, then smiled. "Oh, hi Adam. You're here." Her words came out slurred while she tried to reach for him.

He pushed her back in the seat. "Don't move from this chair until you have had some coffee."

"I don't want any coffee." She attempted to stand.

Adam applied slight pressure on her shoulder and she plopped back, closing her eyes.

"You either drink coffee and sober up or, I'll call a cab to take you home. Which will it be?"

Her head bobbled while she tried to think and look up at Adam at the same time. "You're a spoilsport. I'll-I'll drink the coffee."

"Good."

The waiter was back and handed her the cup, holding the coffee pot in his other hand.

Adam didn't budge until she'd drunk half and was working on the remainder.

"Fill her cup up again when she's finished with that one. And don't allow her to leave here without a designated driver." He turned to me. "Let's get out of here. We've stayed long enough."

"Are you sure?" I grinned up at him, took my thumb and began rubbing off the two smeared red lips on his cheek. "I don't know about you, but I was just beginning to enjoy myself."

"Yeah, I bet you were. I saw your look when she wrapped herself around me."

"I was in shock, nothing more." I shrugged.

He laughed. "For a second there, I thought you were going to tear her off of me."

His arm around my waist, he pulled me into his side, his eyes serious.

"There isn't one woman here, or anywhere on earth for that matter, that can hold a candle to you. And like that old song says, *I only have eyes for you* ... that's me where you're concerned."

Chapter 24

Tonight was the night. One quick run-through, the performance at seven, and then the children's Christmas pageant would be history. After that, all that was left was Christmas with the families and then our wedding. Butterflies took flight in my stomach.

I didn't have long to wait—six more days—before I became Mrs. Adam Ryder. After that, everything would settle back to normal, whatever normal was, because I had completely forgotten how it felt.

I looked forward to the moment I would say "I do." It was getting harder to part from Adam at the end of the day. And lying around on the beach on some tropical island was sounding better and better by the minute.

Arriving at the church early, I ensured everything was ready for the play. Adam was coming later.

The whimsical, almost Charlie Brown-like plywood cutout caricatures of a donkey, cow, and a few sheep were placed around the barn-like lean-to. The manger, center stage, held a baby doll wrapped in a cotton cloth. Hay was scattered around the platform floor, and we had placed a bale of hay for Mary to sit on.

The backdrop was painted to resemble a midnight blue sky with a sprinkling of stars and one brilliant pasteboard silvery star hanging from the ceiling over the lean-to.

Satisfied everything was ready, I took a moment to relax and look over my notes for the play.

The energetic kids began trickling in along with some of the mothers. They ignited the atmosphere with their little voices and high-pitched bubbly laughter.

I was glad to see Lori arrive, knowing she would help with the costumes.

"Auntie Whitty." Mandy burst down the aisle and ran onto stage.

I bent down for her little tight neck squeeze.

"Uncle Seth brought me. Mama didn't come."

Seth, looking like he'd rather be anywhere but here, moved to where we stood.

"Sorry, Sis, but I was sent by Shelly. She's waiting on Zack's call. And since she hadn't heard from him in several days, she asked me to take her place. But she'll be here in plenty of time."

"Thanks for coming." I glanced around and saw Lori was having difficulty wrangling Tommy into his costume. "Help Lori. See what you can do to get him dressed."

Seth rolled his eyes. He walked over to the boy, bent down eye-level and said something, and then stood looking down at him.

Tommy immediately began cooperating.

Lori, looking anything but happy, snapped the back of Tommy's tunic. She adjusted and tied a cloth belt around his waist, and then sent him over to where some other kids were. She glared at Seth while saying something to him before walking in my direction.

"Do you know what your brother did?"

"No. I asked him to help you though."

173

"Seth told Tommy if he didn't stop giving me grief, he'd handcuff him and haul him off to jail where he'd never see his mom and dad again."

I kept my laugh to myself, but my grin was harder to conceal. Knowing Seth loved kids and wouldn't harm a hair on their hair, I tried for peacemaker.

"I'm sure the boy knew Seth was teasing."

"Tommy was practically in tears." Lori's cheeks were suffused with red, her eyes snapping. "Give the man something to do, but as far away from the kids and me as possible."

"Something wrong." Seth walked up giving Lori and me a sheepish grin. He knew.

"You. You're what's wrong." Lori turned and walked away.

My brother watched her, a puzzled expression riding his face. "What bur patch did she fall into?"

"I don't believe she liked how you handled Tommy."

The boy under discussion was standing with the other kids as he kept a watchful eye on Seth.

"I only did what you asked."

"You may have, but it was how you went about it that angered Lori."

He cocked a brow, a confident gleam in his eyes. "He got dressed, didn't he?"

Shaking my head, I moved away. "I got to get the rehearsal started. See if you can stay out of trouble."

Seth moved in Lori's direction. She turned her back to him and walked off.

This time I couldn't keep the grin from showing. I believeb that was the first time I'd ever seen my brother snubbed by a woman.

Clapping my hands, I gained the kids attention. The budding idea that Seth and Lori would make a cute couple popped into my head and then popped out as quickly as it came.

"Hey, beautiful, what's got you smiling?"

Adam gave me a peck on the cheek, his touch making me momentarily forget what I was about to do. "I'll tell you later. Right now I've got to get the rehearsal started."

Mandy ran over, her halo askew and one of her angel wings hanging half off. "Hi, Uncle Adam."

"Hi, pumpkin."

She looked at him oddly, wrinkling her nose. "I'm not a pumpkin. I'm an angel."

"Yes, you are, and a beautiful one too."

Lori walked up and gave Adam a hug.

Seth was close behind. He shook hands with Adam, not knowing he'd knocked off Mandy's other wing in the process. "I see your services were commandeered too."

"I volunteered."

"Now look what you've done." Lori dropped to her knees at the same time Seth bent to pick up the wayward wing. Their heads collided.

"Ouch!" Lori rubbed her forehead, glaring at Seth.

"I'm sorry." Seth leaned back, then stood, the angel wing still in his hand.

"Why don't you go someplace where you won't scare kids, tear up costumes, or try to knock someone out?"

Handing Lori the wing, Seth stared at her in disbelief. "I don't scare kids. It wasn't my fault the angel wing wasn't put on properly and already falling off. And that"— he pointed at her head—"was as much your fault as mine." He crossed his arms over is chest. "Oh, I forgot. You're Miss Perfect. You do nothing wrong." Seth huffed loudly, glancing away

Mandy yanked on Seth's hand. "Don't be mad at Lori, Uncle Seth. She's my friend."

He bent eye level with Mandy, smiling. "I'm not angry, sweetie. Lori and I were just talking rather loudly, nothing more."

175

Lori, still on her knees, reattached the wing, ignoring Seth completely.

"There you go." Lori patted Mandy's head. "Go take your place." Lori moved to stand next to her brother. When Seth followed, she crossed her arms giving him a cold shoulder.

Yep. Seth and Lori would be a good match if they could get past their mutual dislike of each other.

The short practice went well. When we were done, I had everyone go back behind the curtain to wait their cue. Between Adam and Seth, they kept the boys under control and reasonably quiet. The Christmas music began playing which meant the program would start in exactly ten minutes.

The children's minister was in place and ready to begin reading his script. I scanned the audience for Shelly. She was sitting close to the front, a few rows back, next to Mom and Dad.

Since the kids ranged from ages four up to eleven, I asked several moms, along with Lori, Seth, and Adam to stay behind stage and on the sidelines to make sure everyone stayed quiet and came in on cue.

The music stopped. I walked out and took my place down front to direct the children. As the play went along, kids, as they are known to do, squirmed, kicked hay around the floor, and one little boy waved at his mom and dad, which brought chuckles from the audience. The shepherds were off to one side sitting on the ground when the angel appeared to them.

"Behold I have tidings of great joy … Unto you this day, a Savior is born …"

The shepherd boys looked astonished while the angel told them the good news and that they were to go to Bethlehem and look for a baby in a manger. All three of the boys got up and ran a circuitous route around the stage. When they received laughter from the audience, they took another lap around before stopping in front of Mary and Joseph.

Two of the boys knelt before the baby in the manger. The third stood there looking down, his brow scrunched up, his lips tight and puckered.

"That ain't no baby Jesus."

"Is too."

"No it ain't. That's a stupid doll."

Simultaneously, the audience burst out laughing. One of the kneeling boys stood and took his shepherd's staff and started whacking the other boy. Seth and Adam came on stage, each grabbing a boy, carrying him off. It took the audience several moments before they quieted down enough for the pageant to continue.

The rest of the play went along without a hitch. Thankfully, we were on the home stretch. All that was left … "Joy To the World," which the kids enjoyed singing.

After the children lined across the stage in their designated places, the pianist played the intro and they began singing. When they had finished the first verse, as was planned, I turned to the audience and motioned for them to stand and sing along with the children.

I heard a collective gasp and then a crash. When I turned to look, the sky backdrop had fallen down over the lean-to. The plywood animals, one by one, slammed to the floor. A cloud of hay and dust filtered through the air, sprinkling over the little actors and the audience in the front rows. At the back of the stage and standing behind what should have been the backdrop, stood Seth with one shepherd and Adam with the other. A drunken star swayed back and forth, then fell to the ground with a clatter.

Adam took the make believe swords away.

Seth grabbed both boys by the nap of the neck. He bent and whispered something in their ear, nodding in the direction of the other kids. Though both boys dragged their feet, they moved up to stand alongside their friends.

The dust finally settled and everyone stopped laughing and coughing. Thankfully, the pianist started "Joy To The World" once again. The audience joined the children, making a lovely ending to the catastrophe minutes before.

When the program was over, the pastor invited everyone to the family center for refreshments. I wanted to duck out the side door, but Adam wouldn't let me.

He put his arm around me, leading me to the hall. "The finale wasn't quite what you wanted, but look on the bright side."

"What bright side?"

"I thought the kids did a great job."

"You're right, they did."

"And the finale will be remembered for some time to come." He chuckled, picking pieces of hay from my hair and off my clothes.

"In fact, there were several proud fathers with a video camera. I'm sure if we ask, they'll be happy to make us a copy, falling star, sky, and all."

"Wow, thanks." I snorted, shaking my head. "I don't want to be reminded."

As we walked into the large reception hall, I turned to Adam. "I guess the upside is the pastor's wife won't ask me to direct another children's pageant."

"You can only hope."

Chapter 25

"It certainly took you long enough to pop the question." Grams winked at Adam. "Our Whitney Ann will make you one fine wife." She moved from the dining table into the living room.

"I couldn't agree with you more." Adam wrapped his arm around my waist as we followed. "I'm glad to know you're in favor of our marriage."

"Why wouldn't I be?" Grams gave him a look as if he were crazy. "I've been saying to Whitney Ann for some time now, that she needed to get married and have babies."

"Grams, please." If I didn't stop her, she would be saying something equally or more embarrassing.

"All's left, is for that scallywag over there to settle down with a good girl." She pointed her bony finger at Seth, who was coming in our direction. "Then I can go on to my great reward, knowing all's well."

"If my getting married is all that's keeping you from meeting your Maker, then you won't be seeing Him anytime soon. I'm not ready for you to go." He grabbed Grams up in a gentle hug, planting a kiss on her forehead.

She shooed him with her hand. "Go on, you rascal, and leave me alone." Grams beamed with his attention. She moved to the rocker and sat down. Her cheeks turned a beautiful shade of pink as she smoothed her dress down around her legs.

Seth brought over an ottoman, lifting her feet and gently placing her heels on the cushion.

"Go on, now. Stop fussing over me. I'm fine."

"You're the only sweetheart I have to fuss over."

"And whose fault is that?" Grams raised her brows, giving Seth a beady-eyed stare. "You could have a young pretty thing if you'd just settle down."

He shook his head. "Grams, you know I'm not one for settling down. My job's too dangerous to be married. I don't want my wife worrying I might not come home."

"That's an excuse, not a reason. Change what you do. Or better yet, ask the good Lord to find you a woman who has the stomach for your job and to keep you safe ta'boot."

Seth laughed. "Never gonna happen."

"Never say never. Cause in my years of experience, that's when what you fear most will overtake you—in your case it's falling in love with a pretty little gal."

Grams had everyone laughing while Seth rolled his eyes. "Not happenin'."

He meandered over to the tree while everyone found seats around the living room. Mandy, excitement oozing from her pores, sat next to her mother, bouncing. She was more than ready for the presents to be handed out.

Seth began digging out the gifts from beneath the tree. I turned to Adam. "Save my seat." Then I motioned for Mandy to follow me. "Mandy, you're big enough this year to come help me pass out the gifts."

She came running, a smile bigger than Christmas on her face.

I handed her a package. "This one is Papa's."

Each time I handed her a gift, her little legs would pump as fast as they could go, delivering presents around the room.

A knock on the door had everyone looking at the entrance, puzzled. Dad started to get up. I motioned for him to stay seated. "I'll see who it is."

When I opened the door, a cold breeze rushed in. The sight of my brother-in-law Zack brought tears to my eyes. I knew what this would mean to Mandy and Shelly, not to mention the rest of us.

He put his fingers over my mouth to keep me from squealing.

I hugged him up tight, thrilled he'd made it home safe. With a million questions on the tip of my tongue, I motioned him into the living room. This was by far the greatest gift of all—Zack home in time for Christmas to celebrate with the family. Thankfully, our prayers were answered.

A collective gasp bounced around the room.

Shelly turned to look.

Zack, behind her, leaned down and gave her a kiss.

"Daddy." Mandy's scream filled the room. She dropped the package in her hand and ran to him, her arms outstretched.

Zack scooped his daughter up in his arms, burying his face in her golden curls, hugging her fiercely. Continuing to hold Mandy, he slipped in beside his wife. The three of them huddled together in a collective hug, not wanting anything to separate them.

When I sat down on the edge of my seat next to Adam, he leaned in.

"I assume that's Zack."

Wiping my cheek, I nodded, grabbing hold of Adam's hand. "You assume correctly. We weren't expecting him until March or April."

After a zillion questions were asked and answered, everyone settled down again. I made my introduction of Zack to Adam and saw Zack's teasing glint.

"You sure do things fast."

"No use wasting time when you find a good woman." Adam hugged me.

Seth and I resumed handing out the gifts. I didn't think Mandy would leave her father's lap, but she scooted down and looked up at her daddy.

"I'm big now, Daddy."

"I can see that." Zack tweaked Mandy's nose. "I think you've grown two or three inches since the last time I saw you."

Mandy puffed out her chest and nodded. "Auntie Whitty said I was big enough to pass the presents."

"Wow. You are big." He smiled at his daughter, the sparkle of tears in his eyes.

"I'll be back."

She ran over to where I sat on the floor by the tree. I handed her a present, and told her who it belonged to. She glanced at her daddy, wanting him to see her important job, before handing the gift to Grams.

After everyone had received their packages, Mandy sat at her daddy's feet and began pulling at the wrappings on her gifts, making sure Zack saw each present before moving on to the next.

My gift to Adam was warm-ups for exercising. Not expecting a gift from him, he surprised me with a strand of pearls.

"Oh, Adam, they're beautiful. Would you?" I held out the pearls and turned my back to him, lifting my hair.

He clasped the strand around my neck. Before I could lower my hair, he sealed his mission with a kiss on my neck, sending chills of delicious feelings spiraling down my back.

Being married to this man would never be boring. However, waiting two days to belong to Adam Ryder, in every sense of the word, would be two long agonizing days of torture.

Chapter 26

Since all of Adam's relatives had already received invitations to our wedding by mail, they weren't surprised to see me at the family gathering. The only one who acted cool toward me was Brittney, which I somewhat expected.

Again, Lori acted as my buffer. She wouldn't allow Brittney anywhere near me without being there too. Lori kept the conversation going, or she'd ask me to come help her with some fictitious job.

Adam and Michael seemed to get along well, almost back to normal, by what Lori told me. I hoped one day in the near future, Brittney would come around and try to make peace also, to which Lori told me not to hold my breath.

The date for our wedding was discussed. Someone mentioned that it was a bit hasty.

"I'm surprised he didn't take Whitney off to Vegas." Jim raised his brows smiling. "That's what Dad and I did with our brides."

"Oh, believe me, I tried." Adam winked at me. "Whitney wouldn't have it. So we compromised with a quickly planned wedding."

"Well, tomorrow isn't that far off now." Jim stood glancing around. "I don't know about anyone else, but I'm all for snagging another piece of Audrey's apple pie."

Others followed, effectively cutting off the discussion.

"You want a piece?" Adam stood, looking down at me.

"No. If I eat another bite, I won't be able to fit into my dress tomorrow."

He squeezed my hand. "Then I'll be right back."

Michael and Lori followed him. They were talking and laughing as they left the room.

Only a few were left in the living room. And since they were holding their own conversation, I leaned my head back and closed my eyes. The tiredness of the last few weeks had taken its toll.

The cushion next to me dipped, and thinking I would see Adam, I opened my eyes, smiling.

Brittney. I cringed inside, not wanting a sparring match or a heated discussion.

"Hi, Brittney. You didn't want any pie either?"

"I'm not here to discuss pie. I'm here to talk about Adam."

"What about him." I moved over in the loveseat, angling my body so I could face her and gain some distance between us.

"You may have everyone in this family convinced Adam loves you, but I don't believe he does."

The racing of my heart had the blood pounding through my veins making me a little light headed. I didn't want to argue with Brittney, yet I didn't want her thinking Adam had any feelings left for her.

"I won't debate the merits of Adam's love for me or mine for him. What I will say, no matter what you think you know, this time tomorrow it will be a moot issue. Adam and I will be married. We plan for our marriage to last a lifetime. So get over Adam, if that is what this jealousy is all about.

I took a deep breath, praying for the right words for healing. "You have a husband that adores and loves you. He would do anything to make you happy, if you'll let him."

"How dare you tell me how to live. You don't know a thing about me or Michael."

"True." I turned my hands over in supplication, hoping to get through to Brittney. "Listen, far be it for me to tell you or anyone else how to live. All I know is Michael will make you happy. Give him a chance to show you how much you mean to him."

"What has Adam told you about us?"

"Only that you and he dated for a short period of time. And then you dated Michael and married him."

Tears were at the brink of pouring over Brittney's lashes. "No one understands. Everyone thinks I don't love Michael, but I do. They think I married him on the rebound." She sniffed, swiping at her cheek. "Which might have been partly true in the beginning, but not now. He's good to me."

I touched her hand. When she didn't flinch or pull back, I felt it was a good sign.

"It doesn't matter what others think. It only matters what you feel for your husband inside here." I tapped my heart.

Brittney sniffed again, nodding.

"I would like for us to be friends, if not now, maybe one day in the near future."

"What are you two in deep discussion about?" Adam moved over next to me, placing his hand on my shoulder, his eyes mirroring concern as he studied me to see if I was upset.

I hoped he knew how much I loved him. "Nothing. Just girl talk. You'd be bored stiff within a minute."

Adam narrowed his gaze, weighing my words. "Then I won't ask." He smiled. "We have a big day tomorrow, and I think we should be heading back."

"I think you're right. There are a few last minute things I need to do before tomorrow." I turned to Brittney. "After the wedding and once we're settled in, we'd love to have Michael and you over for dinner."

"Really?" Her face showed disbelief. "I'd-we'd like that." For the first time she gave me a genuine smile, looking relieved.

"Good." I stood, facing Adam. "I'm ready if you are."

As we said our goodbyes, Grandpa Ryder gave me a hug and a peck on the cheek. "I knew Adam wouldn't let you get away." He winked at me. "He's smarter than that."

"For a while, there were a few dicey moments as to whether she'd say yes." Adam's arm wound around my waist, pulling me closer. "But it was worth every anxious moment when she finally did."

We left the house and hurried out to the car. I hopped inside quickly to get out of the freezing wind.

Adam turned on the engine, and allowed the car to idle. He took my hand and pulled me toward him. "Come here. I've been wanting to do this all day."

Dipping his head, he gave me a mind-blowing kiss, leaving my emotions reeling.

Leaning his forehead against mine, he blew out a breath. "I'm sure glad we're getting married tomorrow. Otherwise, I don't think I could take many more days being without you—you going to your apartment and me to mine. That's pure torture."

I laughed as he leaned back in his seat.

"It's no laughing matter." He put the car in gear, backing out of the driveway. "I go crazy every time I have to leave you, knowing I can't be with you, holding you in my arms."

I knew how he felt. Each night grew harder when he got up to leave, closing the door that separated us.

Adam maneuvered the car down the road heading back to our apartments. "After tomorrow you'll be like my platinum card."

I looked at him strangely while he chuckled.

"I won't leave home without you."

Chapter 27

"Your gown is absolutely perfect."

Sally zipped the back of my dress, while I sucked in my breath.

"I know, isn't it?" Tiffany lifted my veil off the hanger and began fluffing the flimsy, flyaway material.

"Yeah, but one more dinner and slice of pie and I wouldn't have been able to fit into the thing."

The door opened after a light tap. My mother's head peeked in. "I wanted to make sure you're decent before walking in."

"I am. Come on." I motioned, turning to face her.

Mom, Grams, and Aunt Polly each took turns giving me a hug. They *oohed* and *aahed* over my appearance.

Grams held out a lacy white hankie. "I wasn't sure if you had something borrowed, so I brought this one, just in case."

"I didn't. That's so sweet. Thank you, Grams." I kissed her cheek then tucked the hankie inside my sleeve at my wrist.

"And here is something blue." Aunt Polly held out a blue ribbon. "Where's your bouquet?"

"Over here." Sally lifted the lid to the box.

"They're absolutely beautiful." My aunt sniffed the bouquet before tying the blue ribbon around the holder.

"Thanks, Aunt Polly." I looked at mom expectantly. "Where's Shelly? Isn't she here yet?" I turned to face Tiffany, ducking down so she could place my veil over my head.

As I turned to face the others in the room, I noticed my mom worrying her lower lip. A queasy feeling erupted in my stomach.

"She was feeling a little under the weather this morning."

"No. She can't be. She's supposed to be my matron of honor. We had a bargain. She'd be in my wedding. I'd be her birthing coach." I knew I sounded like a lunatic, but if she were having labor pains, I didn't want to miss the birth of my nephew, and I didn't want my sister missing my wedding.

"I don't think she's going into labor. When last I spoke with her, she was beginning to feel better and said they would be here shortly." Again she worried her lower lip.

"What else aren't you telling me?" I looked at her suspiciously.

"Well, your dad told me not to tell you. It would just upset you."

"Now you're really scaring me. Out with it. I won't be upset, or least I hope I won't. "

"Well, it's the cake."

"What about the cake?" This time a hornets' nest took flight in my stomach.

"The top layer on your cake teetered off and fell, making a small indentation in the other layers."

"What?" Nearly in tears, I was ready to run out of the room and check the damage. "How'd it happen?"

"We don't know. Either someone bumped into the table, or the dowels weren't put in properly. Not sure. But don't worry. Adam called the bakery. They're here now repairing the damage."

Not feeling completely satisfied with Mom's answer, yet knowing there wasn't a thing I could do about it, I finished dressing. I pulled out the pearls Adam gave me for Christmas and latched them around my neck. My nervous fingers gently ran over the strand. The pearls, already warmed from my skin, calmed me some.

"Mandy. What about Mandy? If Shelly gets sick again, Zack will drop her off, won't he? She has to be here. She's my flower girl."

Mom gave me a tentative smile. "Since they haven't called, I'm sure they're on their way. She'll be here—"

"Aunt Whitty." The little bundle of joy burst through the door, her curls bouncing. "Look at my dress." She held out the skirt, turning in circles. "It's like Mommy's."

She stopped to stare at me. Her little mouth open. "Are you a princess?"

Her words chased the worries away and brought about a smile. "No. This is my wedding dress."

"When I get big, I'm gonna wear a dress just like that." She touched it, running her little fingers over the pearls and sequins.

Another knock came from the door. "Are you decent in there?" Zack's voice carried from out in the hall.

"She's decent." Mom pulled open the door.

Zack and Shelly came into the room. He looked handsome in his dress uniform. Shelly appeared a little tired but very beautiful and very pregnant. She seemed to perk up when she saw me. "You make a beautiful bride."

"How are you feeling?" I prayed she'd say fine as I ran my hand over her belly and the little guy who had given me a scare. He kicked, and we both laughed.

"Good enough to get this show on the road." Shelly patted her belly. "This little guy is anxious to see his father. But not until after the wedding."

"Keep telling little Zack that while you walk down the aisle." I paused. "Maybe you should sit down during the ceremony instead of standing with the wedding party."

"No. I'll be fine."

Another knock was heard.

"This is becoming Grand Central Station." I laughed nervously.

Mom did the honors again. This time she spoke to the person on the other side and then turned motioning for Grams and Aunt Polly. "They're wanting us in the vestibule. It's time for the family to be seated and the wedding to begin."

"Zack, if you wouldn't mind doing the honor of escorting Aunt Polly, Grams, and Mom down the aisle to their seat, it would make me very happy."

"Sure, my pleasure." He kissed Shelly, then placed Gram's arm in his. "Shall we go, ladies?"

Thankfully, with the rehearsal last Wednesday and a dinner afterward, everyone knew where to go, what to do, and when to do it. Zack was the only switch up. However, I knew he'd make an excellent addition to our wedding.

Dad came in all misty-eyed, clearing his throat. "Like your mother, you make a beautiful bride."

"Thanks, Daddy." I kissed his cheek.

"Are you sure about Adam?"

"Absolutely."

I didn't take offense at his question because I knew he had my interest at heart. I patted his arm. "I've never been more sure about anything in my life. There isn't another man on earth that I could love more than I do him."

He cleared his throat. "That's all I wanted to hear. Let's get this wedding started."

As we stood outside in the vestibule of the church waiting for our cue, the music played in the background. I rehearsed in my mind how, for over two years, Adam and I passed in the hall, not recognizing we were meant to be together. Yet, if I hadn't needed a date and been so upset over not having one, I would have missed a chance in a lifetime to meet and marry this remarkable man.

I closed my eyes thanking God for placing Adam on the balcony that night.

The intro to the wedding march sounded. Dad placed my arm through his.

"You ready?"

I nodded unable to speak. My knees felt weak. My heart began pounding like there was no tomorrow. Yet when I saw Adam standing down front alongside the minister and the rest of the wedding party, smiling, my nerves settled down.

Walking down the aisle, I saw red rose petals on the carpet and gave a sigh of relief. That was before I noticed a woman picking petals out of her cleavage, and another one, petals from her hair. When we passed a man brushing petals off his suit, I knew what had happened.

Mandy.

The little stinker was grinning and waving at me. I couldn't help but smile back at her.

Shelly said something in her ear. My niece stopped, puckering her face into a frown, her lips buried in a straight line. I smiled at her. She perked up and started grinning.

Adam stepped forward.

Dad kissed my cheek. "Be happy."

"I will."

"Her mother and I give you Whitney." He placed my hand in Adam's warm palm. "All we ask in return is that you love and treasure her as much as we do."

"I will and I do." Adam was looking at me when he answered.

We turned to stand in front of Pastor Steve. He motioned for everyone to be seated. He spoke on the merits of marriage and love, and our responsibility to one another.

When it came time for Adam to slip the ring on my finger, he spoke the traditional vows.

"For better for worse, for richer or poorer, in sickness and in health, until death us do part." His eyes looked deep into mine. "Whitney, you are my heart, my soul, and I love you with every fiber of my being. I pledge to love, protect, and cherish you for the rest of my life."

Shelly stepped up. I handed her my bouquet and she handed me Adam's ring. My hands shook so much I nearly dropped my token of love for Adam. My efforts to push the metal over his knuckle met with resistance before making it all the way on his finger. And though I remembered saying the vows at the appropriate time, everything went by in a blur.

"I now pronounce you man and wife." Pastor Steve smiled. "You may kiss your bride."

Adam lifted my veil and pulled me in his arms. He kissed me like there was no tomorrow.

"Oh, no."

The gasp had us both turning to look at Shelly who was clutching her stomach.

"Zack!" Shelly stared at her husband.

Murmurs grew from the congregation.

Adam and I moved to Shelly's side.

"Zack, get the car. Your baby doesn't want to wait." Her face red, her eyes filled with tears and pain, she handed me my bouquet. "I'm sorry, but I did warn you. Ooo-ooo-ooo."

All bedlam broke loose.

Zack ran out of the church.

Mom and Dad, rushed up, one on each side of Shelly. They helped her down the aisle and out of the doors while everyone stood frozen, watching the drama play out.

Looking a little shocked, Pastor Steve turned and smiled. "Well, that's a first."

The audience laughed.

Adam looked at me. "Are you ok?"

"I'm fine. I can't say she didn't warn me."

"We have another thing that people will be discussing for some time to come—our wedding" He winked at me.

Pastor Steve cleared his throat, gaining everyone's attention. "If you will, please say a prayer for Shelly and her little one, who was gracious enough to wait until the ceremony was over."

Another rumble of laughter rose then subsided.

He motioned for Adam and me to turn around. "Now I would like to present to you Mr. and Mrs. Adam Ryder."

Everyone clapped while the organist struck up the wedding recessional.

Knowing it was our cue, Adam took my free hand, leading me out of the sanctuary.

"That was close." I chewed my lip, wondering if I should go to the hospital.

"Too close, if you ask me." Adam chuckled then sobered. "What's up?"

"I was supposed to be her birthing coach."

"Zack is here. And no offense, but I'm sure she would much rather have her husband at her side."

"You're right." I leaned into Adam, hoping some of his strength would rub off on me."

"No. Stop it." Mandy's angry voice had me searching for her.

She shoved the ring bearer and then came running over to me, hiding behind the skirt of my dress. "He says I'm his bride, and he's taking me home. I don't want to go with him. Do I have to?"

Trying my best not to laugh, I looked down at her. "No Mandy. You didn't get married to Brandon. Your Uncle Adam and I were the ones who got married. You were the flower girl. Brandon was the ring bearer. Nothing more." I patted her head. "Now go stand by Nana while we greet our

195

guests. We'll be eating soon. And, shh"—I put my finger to my lips—"don't tell anyone. There's cake for dessert."

Mandy stuck her tongue out at little Brandon, then swayed like a princess over to her grandparents.

"You handled that well, wife."

I shook my head. "Let's just hope no more problems turn up. I don't think I could handle another." My shoulders slumped as I released a heavy breath. "If I survive today …"

"Think blue skies, warm sand, and a soft gentle breeze coming off the ocean with only you and me." Adam pulled me up tight against his side.

"At this moment, I'd welcome a shack in the piney woods of Texas." I glanced up at him, a smile on my lips. "Can we leave now?"

"No can do. But soon."

Chapter 28

A warm breeze blew across my toasty skin with the smell of the ocean filtering through the air. I buried my feet deeper in the sand loving the feel of the salty granules between my toes.

In my dreamy state, it felt like light-years away from our wedding, yet it had only been ten days. Ten blissful days of happiness and love since I had walked down the aisle and said I do to Adam ... *my Adam*. I was blessed above all women.

A shadow blocked the sun and droplets of water shimmied across my skin. Two cool lips joined mine, giving me a salty kiss, curling my toes.

"Hey, you. Are you ready to go back to the room and pack?" Adam looked so good in his swim trunks.

I shielded my eyes as I watched him plop down beside me on the blanket towel, one I had purchased as a souvenir of Kauai. Though, I didn't need a souvenir to remember the heavenly days and nights I had spent with Adam on the small island.

"Can't we buy a place and live here indefinitely?"

Laughing, he tweaked my nose. "Sure, if you find a buried treasure."

"Spoilsport." I rolled on my side to look at my husband. "Hmm, in that case I guess we'll have to pack."

Rivulets of water rolled down Adam's face as sparkling drops glistened in his hair. He looked rested and relaxed with his hands behind his head, eyes closed.

Needing to touch him, I trailed my finger across his chest. I never tired of the feel of him or the reality that I was married to this incredible man who seemed to anticipate my every need.

Squinting, he grabbed my arm, kissed my fingers, and then held my hand next to his heart.

I felt his rapid heartbeat, thrilled that I, not his swim in the ocean, had something to do with its increase.

"When we get home—"

"Yours or mine?" I grinned, feeling playful.

Numerous times over the last ten days we had discussed how one of us would have to put our things in storage. Neither apartment could accommodate more furnishings.

Releasing my hand, he put his arms behind his head again, eyes closed. "Yours, probably. But either works for me."

I ran my finger across his brow, wiping back the cute unruly hair that hung down over his right eye.

"If you don't stop that, I won't be responsible." His lips turned up into a sexy grin, his dimples warming my insides.

Dipping my finger into one of his dimples, I sighed, "Ok, but what fun is there in stopping?"

He growled, rolled to face me, and then kissed me senseless. When he was through he grabbed a strand of my hair and breathed in deeply.

"Mm, I can't get enough of you. I love your smell and how you feel in my arms when I hold you. Just looking at you drives me crazy." He nibbled on my neck then pulled back. "But this is neither the time or place."

Dropping the strand of hair, he propped his head in his hand. "I would like to discuss something with you."

"Ooo, you sound so serious."

"This is serious."

"Now you have my attention."

"For Christmas I received a hefty bonus from work."

"That's nice. Maybe I'll go shopping and buy you something." I ran my fingers through his hair.

"Do you want to hear what I have to say, or do you want me to kiss you senseless again?" His sexy dimples appeared.

"If I have to pick, I'll take the last one."

"After I tell you my plans."

I nipped his lips playfully before giving him a kiss.

Pulling back, I smiled at him. "That'll tide me over. I'm all ears."

He rolled his eyes, smiling at my antics. "If you are in agreement—"

"I'm always in agreement with you."

"Stop interrupting."

"My lips are sealed." I zipped my fingers across my mouth, tightly pressing my lips together.

"I'll bet they are." He chuckled. "Anyway, I thought we would go house hunting when we got back to Dallas.

"House hunting? Are you serious? Can we—"

"Zip it till I'm through." He gave me a stern look then spoiled it by smiling.

I made the sound and motion of zipping my lips again.

"You're impossible." His eyes sparkled. "But I love you anyway,"

"Good to know. Because I love you most."

He shook his head, a playful glint in his eyes.

"As I was about to say, the bonus will make a nice down payment for a house in a respectable area. Nothing too fancy. But it will be our home and a place to start a family. What do you think?"

Stunned in a good way, I was speechless, never thinking we could afford a home for several years to come. The possibilities were endless ... including children.

"You can unzip it now." Adam looked a little concerned. "Say something."

"Oh, Adam ..." Tears came to my eyes. "That would be wonderful, if you're sure you don't want to spend your bonus in some other way."

"It's our bonus. Remember that. And I can't think of anything that would make me happier than for us to be in our own home, just the two of us"—he wiggled his brows—"and eventually the patter of little feet would be nice, if we're blessed."

"Then I say yes."

We continued discussing where to buy and the possibility of finding the right home for the right price, knowing the cost of houses in Dallas was rising as we spoke.

The ride to the airport and flight home were bittersweet. Our idyllic days on Kauai had come to an end and were stored in my memory to pull out and enjoy over and over. I thought of that fateful night in November when Adam came to my rescue yet, shuddered to think what would have happened if I'd turned him down. Knowing Adam as I did now, I would like to believe somehow he would have devised a plan to get us together.

Of all the memories stored away, one would never die or get old in my heart and mind—the day I said *I do* and became Mrs. Adam Ryder.

Other Books By Janice Olson

Romantic Suspense:
The Texas Sorority Sisters Series
Book 1 - Serenity's Deception
Book 2 - Lethal Intent
Book 3 - Chameleon
Book 4 - Run … You Can't Hide
Book 5 - The Collector – *Release 2016*
Romance with a twist of humor:
Texas Serendipity Series
Mr. What's-His-Name
Wanted A Man For Christmas
Airtight Case For Love - (Seth & Lori's story)
Release February 1, 2016

Scheduled For 2016 & 2017
The McCaslands—Tying the Knot
Hope, Texas
5-book romance series over the course of 2016 & 2017

Garrett, Justin, Nick, and Matt are self-appointed protectors of their baby sister, Allyson (Ally). In their opinion, no man is good enough for their sister. They want to protect her from all the handsome wolves that also come knocking on her door.

Ally wants to be left in peace to date whomever she pleases. Instead, her dates are often persuaded to leave the house without her. She has devised a plan to accomplish her goal. Marry off her loveable, but pesky brothers.

Let the fun begin!
Book 1 – Garrett McCasland – Bushel Of Love
Book 2 – Justin McCasland – Love Found in Hope
Book 3 –Nicholas (Nick) McCasland – Trouble With Love
Box 4 – Matthew (Matt) McCasland –Love Drops In
Book 5 –Allison (Ally) McCasland – Free to Pursue Love

From Janice Olson:

I hope you enjoyed Whitney's story.

Believe it or not, my husband asked me to marry him after two weeks of dating. Of course, unlike Whitney and Adam, we didn't. However, we were married a little over a year later. Fun times. ☺

As Whitney, I've been faced with situations where someone is in my face or, as my friend, Michelle, would say, all up in my business. For whatever reason, they don't like me or they choose to cause trouble. When this happens, I want to react, but not in a good way.

I'm reminded what Proverbs 15:1 says … *a gentle answer turns away wrath.* In Whitney's case, it seems to have worked. It's also worked for me too.

Until next time, may all your problems be found in a book.

Janice

Mailing Address:
Janice Olson
P.O. Box 382380
Duncanville, Texas 75132
or
Email: Janice@JaniceOlson.com

I would love to hear from you and if you enjoyed the book. And as always, if you find errors in the book, please notify me so I may make the corrections for everyone's better enjoyment.

And as I respect your time, please respect mine. No junk mail please. ☺